SHADOWS OF AIR AND EARTH

By B.K. Cavaleri

Contact: www.bkcavaleri.com

Cover Art: The Red Fox Creative

Watercolor Map Art: B. K. Cavaleri

Primary Editor: Sarah Anacker

Secondary Editor: Megan Long

First Edition: February 2025

10 9 8 7 6 5 4 3 2 1

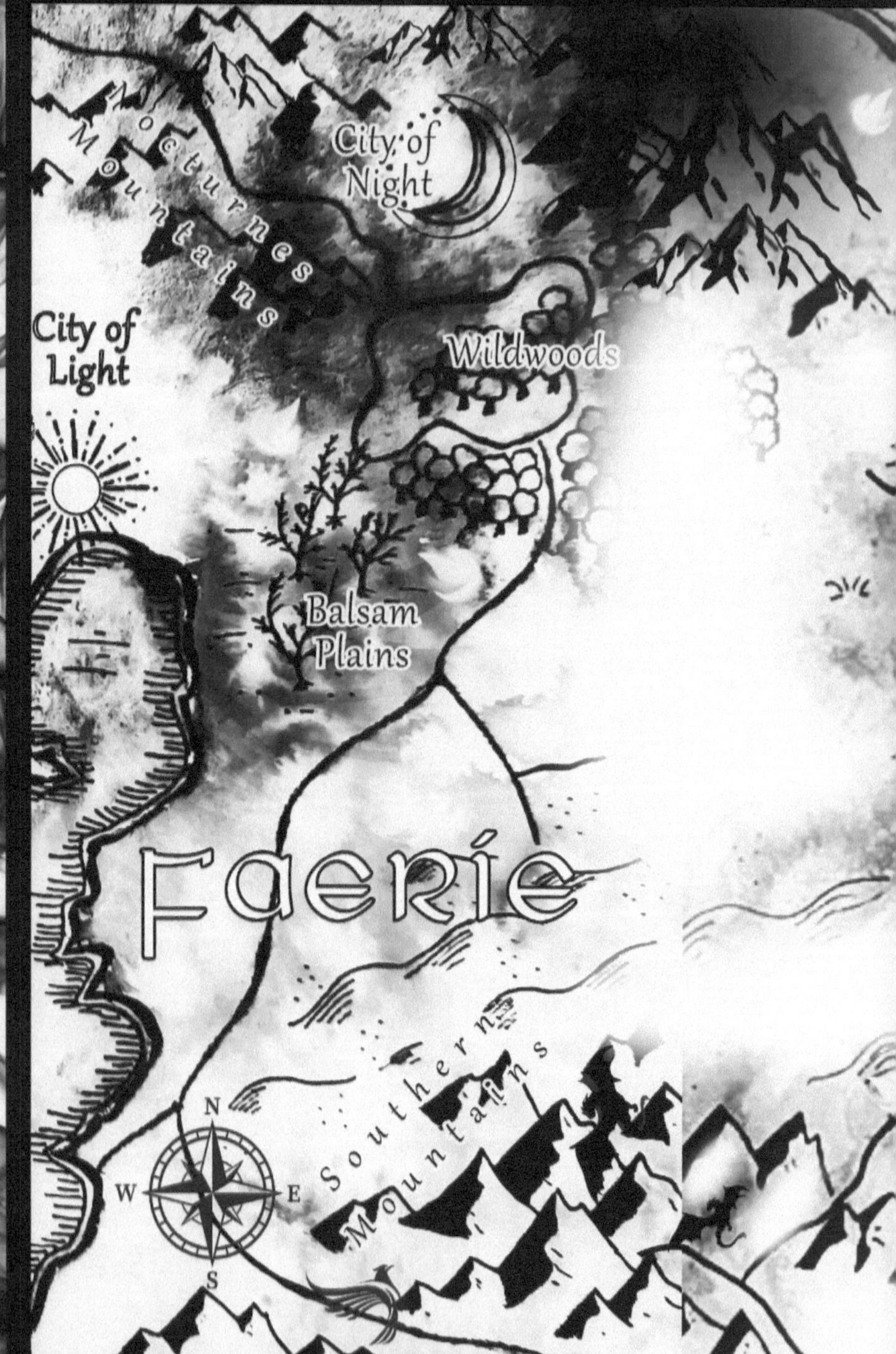

Nocturnes Mountains
City of Night
City of Light
Wildwoods
Balsam Plains
Faerie
N
W
E
S
Southern Mountains

Goddess River
Croi
Pluma Cove
The Veil
elemental plains
Lac Asrai
Saltu
Lacail

Shadows of Air and Earth

Remnant Archives A Novella

By B.K. Cavaleri

 Evangeline Press

CONTENT & TRIGGER WARNINGS

This is a dark fantasy romance with themes of language, violence, mentioning of child abuse, sexual assault, mentioning of rape, paternal death, themes of bound captivity, and premise of infertility complications. For readers 18+.

DEDICATION

For the ***besties*** that will throat punch a bitch, bury a body without question, and safeguard their friend's hearts from ever being broken.
You are
Amici anime. Friends of the soul.

PROLOGUE

Two Hundred Years Post Blood Wars

I LICKED MY LIPS nervously, my white hair catching on the damp moisture for the hundredth time while I waited. A nervous habit I could not stop, especially not tonight. This was the craziest shit we have ever decided to do and I fucking hated being out of my comfort zone.

Blowing the strands from my lips, I surveyed the parade from the marble statue garden, where I hid, cocooned in their stoney embrace. Calm, solid, the statues were the opposite of the spectacle I watched from within the shadows.

Faerie's capital gleamed with all its splendor in decorations of white and silver. A full blown revelry in honor of the winter solstice that did not hold back in its jollification of our sacred holiday. Elemental and water fae performed dazzling displays of power and showmanship, but it was all a ruse. Because what lurked beneath the carousing surface of this pristine city was something much darker. Traitors to the throne hung decaying upon the city's gates, the neglected outside streets festered with greed and desperation, and deep within the courts, whispers stirred of a power that no fae had ever seen before.

It was goddess damn dangerous to be here even hidden within the stones that I found peace and solace in.

Tainted by fear and paranoia, the City of Light had been this way ever since the Blood Wars ended—ever since Deirdre Tatianna Maeve Seelie was crowned queen.

Ripped apart and full of distrust throughout her rule, the elemental and water fae courts bled in silence. Only the shifter and shadow fae courts seemed to come out unscathed. King Asher of The West Isles kept his people safe across the great seas where leagues of water and the illusive Shen's wall divided our worlds. But even that would not stop the queen. It was only a matter of time. He would be a fool to think otherwise. Secret whisperings of the inner court told of future war, plans of expanding the rule of Deirdre's crown over The West Isles.

That wasn't the only stirrings heard. It was said that Eve, lady of the shadow fae court had been ignoring Deirdre's summons for years, refusing to tithe to the queen. As such, there was not a single shadow fae left in the City of Light.

Except for one...Remnant Ezra Solaire Dark.

The powerful general of the Faerie throne wielded shadows like the death god wielded the reaping. She was fearfully respected and respectfully feared by all. It was said the depths of her emerald green eyes could read one's innermost thoughts and see their true intentions like the shifter king of old, and if she deemed them unworthy...her shadows would make sure not even Sheol found their soul.

And for the love of the goddess, she was the *exact* reason why I was here and yet...she had not arrived.

Shifting nervously, I licked my lips again. She was supposed to be here, making sure her queen was protected on the day of the Winter Solstice. The queen held this event yearly and like the sharpness of a blade always tended to, so was her weapon of a general, like a decoration on her arm. I knew this for a solid fact since we had scouted out this despicable event for the past five fucking years.

Five years was nothing in the world of the fae but for our needs, it was a goddess damn lifetime. We could not mess this up...it was *vital* we did not mess this up or it would be our bodies swaying in the soft spiritual breeze of Faerie's winter winds.

A roaring cheer tore up from the crowd and I searched frantically for the cause of the sound. Blowing out my hair softly, I uncovered my face from the shield the white tresses provided. I always hid half my face. I hated it when people fucking stared and unfortunately, my face drew way too much attention. I'd much rather be the rock hidden deep beneath the earth, where my power was grounded and safe. Steady and unwavering, the earth was always there, always true to what really mattered in this damaged world.

Seeing now with both my eyes, relief and trepidation coursed through my veins while I watched shadows roll in across the diamond carved platform where the Queen of Faerie stood. Remnant Dark had arrived and the fae rejoiced. Standing next to the queen, together they were pulled through the streets by a team of twenty silver prancing unicorns, their hooves clacking upon the stone and crushing the red strewn flower petals in their wake. Not to be outdone by land, an ostentatious display of pixies zipping through the air blasted brightly colored fireworks of dust, painting Faerie's enchanting dark skies where the three moons glowed.

All this for the silver splendor of the Faerie Queen, a fae that was rotten on the inside despite her beauty.

I held back my gag at the way Dierdre stood waving, her aquamarine eyes shining with narcissistic enjoyment. To complete her look, a garish crown adorned her head in a filagree of silver and diamonds, the obnoxious display adding to her own conceited vanity.

But the fae were not watching her, despite her outdone splendor. No. All eyes were on the shadow fae standing just slightly at her back, toned tattooed arms tucked behind her, her black and blue hair unbound and flowing just like the dark shadows that billowed in waves beneath her feet. Dressed in black with only a chest plate of silver armor and a silver-plated sword sheathed at her side, she was beauty and power wrapped in a stunning package that the queen could never stand up to even if she wore all the jewels in the world.

My lips thinned. Not understanding why the general was so dotingly devoted to the disgusting fae beside her. It was a weakness we would be taking full advantage of tonight, especially since the shadow fae general was hypervigilant in her duty to protect her queen amongst the obnoxious mob. Emerald eyes focused on every single one of the adoring fans, scanning for threats while her features stayed smooth and calm, not giving even a fraction of a thought away. But I was no fool, I had seen her in action before and despite her relaxed stance, she was poised...ready.

But so were we. *Five years ready.*

"She's here Ri," I whispered to the soft breeze blowing across my face. Riley's breeze. I would know his elemental air anywhere.

"I'm in," his voice whispered into my ear even though he was nowhere near close to me. I glanced up at the looming palace basking me in its dark shadows where he hid within. Wishing I could see him. But the only thing I saw was a lone snowy white owl hunting the palace's dark corners for its next meal.

Pulling my gaze away and feeling acutely worried, I kept my eyes steady on the general, knowing she could disappear before a fae blinked and that—that would be their cold end. Faster than any shadow fae I had ever known, she used her darkness with clever deceptivity, sensing dangers and threats like a shifter hunted prey.

Over the past five years of our cautious studying, I've seen her do it dozens of times. The terrifying fact of it was, no one else ever did. Disappearing and reappearing in shadows, she took out fae that were a threat like plucking weeds from a garden. Quietly, unmercifully, without a moment's thought. There one second, gone the next, with one less fae celebrating within the city.

Everytime I observed it, it sent a foreboding chill down my spine...just like it had the first time I had ever seen her power in action during the Night of the Wailing.

Yet, despite my fear...I admired her formidable strength and power. Perhaps in a different lifetime we could have been friends, but her alliance with the queen made that event impossible. Shamefully, she was the hand of the queen of Faerie and as long as that bitch sat on the throne, Remnant Dark would always be my enemy.

Sliding quietly along the marble path to follow the progress of the parade, my elemental power of earth masking any noise of footsteps, I sneaked between another grouping of statues. Like all the others watching, I was still just as entranced as I was aware of the deadly shadow fae general.

Come on Ri, I pleaded silently.

"Got it," whispered his suave tone, the air tickling the shell of my ear and I ignored the way my stomach flipped at the husky whisper. I needed to focus for goddess sakes.

Suddenly, like a fucking cù sìth foretelling death, the general's emerald green eyes cut straight to my darkened hiding place and I inhaled sharply. I knew there was no way she could see me, I was part of the earth, part of the statue I stood by, but it sure as fuck felt like she could.

Sweet goddess and all her shit, I've seen that look before, I hated that look. It meant Remnant Dark had found a new mark and it was now *me*.

An explosion of pixie fireworks suddenly made the crowd roar and her gaze shifted slightly, just enough to release me from my state of panic and split the earth, dropping Riley and me deep beneath the ground, where the tunnels I had carefully carved the past five years lay.

A half scream tore from me when I felt something brush against my side, quickly cut off by air being sucked from my lungs.

"Fuck Xi, it's just me," Riley whispered. Noticing my shoulders slump with relief, he restored my air, leaving me choking while his glowing hazel eyes narrowed on me. I always loved the color of them, like andalusite gems—my favorite stone of browns and greens, like the earth. "What happened up there?"

Tugging my white hair back over my face, I muttered, "She looked right at me Ri. I don't think she saw us but I have a feeling...." I shook my head, cursing.

I could not see his features in the darkness of the tunnel, but I could read the flash of worry in those bright eyes that I adored. "Well in that case, it would be foolish to ignore *feelings* terella." Goddess that whispered air, *his air*, hovering again over the crest of my ear forced a shiver out of me. "Lead us out of here."

I grabbed his shoulder before he turned away, "Did you get it?"

Feeling the warmth of his smile, his breeze whispering gently around my body, he used the air to tuck my hair back from my face, to see both my eyes, something he only did when we were alone. Respecting my need to hide all other times, except from him. I would never hide from him.

I could hear the smile of satisfaction in his low voice, "Yes."

***

Remnant

I knew she was there, she was always there, every year, for the past *five years*. It was never any different. There was no threat, just a careful studying, a studious assessment of the spectacle I wish I never had to be a part of, and the strange quality of her aura. Then the damn pixie fireworks got the crowd so goddess riled up that a few of them got too close to the queen and I had to react.

The moment the crowd calmed, my gaze snapped back to the statues where I knew she hid, except she was now gone. Cursing inwardly, I shook my head.

I could never see her, but I knew she was there...her aura always the same. Pale blue, soothing, and loyal—it shimmered, sparkling like a star in the sky. Intriguing and unique. A quality I never seen before from a fae and because of it, I was always rather eager to see if she would show, likely the only reason I even came to this event these days.

For it definitely was not for the queen, whom I left to get drunk and dance the night away with her spoiled inner court, her newest admirer the commander of the city among them. The Winter Solstice was a celebration of the shortest day of the year, a chance to spread light into the world while darkness descended for the next three months.

It was my favorite time. Except I found I could not celebrate and definitely not with the queen.

Deirdre and I's relationship had been unraveling for the past few years. My intentions in joining her court were to keep my family safe but the vast power we both held brought us together as confidants, and ultimately lovers. I knew I was playing a dangerous game. One of choosing selfish desires brought on by years of loneliness all while keeping my true self, my true motives locked away. Except now the bond I had cultivated, the trust I had gained was growing strained. Deirdre's most recent acts of violence against her own people, driving the distance between us even further. Alarmed, I had voiced my concern, not at all condoning her rash behavior in killing fae that were never proven to be traitors. A stance that she found both amusing and irritating. Stating that I needed to steel my spine and grow up from my mother's shadow if I were to stay by her side and make the hard decisions for the better of Faerie.

For the better of Faerie. That was what I had always been here for and while I was no ancient fae, I knew goddess damn right from wrong. I had always known that there was a piece of the queen that was borderline mad, it was what made me take the vows in the first place. I had sensed danger there, for the fae, for my court, for the world. Except the extent of our powers left us both isolated and lonely in the palace life...I never would have guessed that I would fall in love with her. In that, I had seen a side of her no one else had. Vulnerable and soft, a lover in the darkness that drew me deceptively in.

Clenching my hand at my side, I cursed, sometimes one could not help who they loved. That's what I told myself and while I still did love her, our intimacies had become less and less as of late. Her teasing had become more cruel than seductive. Her touch more possessive than loving. A fact my heart didn't give a shit about as if it were entranced by her, craving the softer fae that I fell in love with.

Stepping from the shadows, having escaped the celebrations where drink and revelry were reaching new heights, I walked along the marble statue garden. A memorial of fae lost in the Blood Wars. Pausing, I looked up at Deirdre's mother, Talgira, carved at the center of the gardens...so much like her daughter but also not. Her face was set outwards, seeing more beyond the horizon than I ever could.

Shivering, I leaned against her side, looking out beyond the City of Light, where her gaze looked knowingly onward toward the seductive waves of the ocean.

"Something is amiss. What do you see that I cannot?" I whispered, the shadows curling up into my arms while I absently watched a lone snowy white owl swoop through the stars heading east, hunting for its prey just as I hunted for answers.

Stroking the shadows, I pursed my lips...fate would unravel soon. I could feel it—just like the cool soothing darkness nestled in my arms. I just had to be patient, and well that...that never was my strongest suit.

CHAPTER 1

"Through the shadows she climbed, racing along the Nocturnes, determined to pull the eternal flame from the nuckelavee in order to stop the plaguing eclipse. A solar disease that had cut the sun from the sky for three long weeks."

The tavern was on edge, their voices hushed, no one moved. Even the bard relinquished his platform listening in, enthralled by *her* stories.

Xi Lanora Chin.

For a fae that did not like attention, she fell into her own when it came to epic tales, especially ones of the great General Remnant Dark. And if one didn't know better, they would have thought that Xi Chin admired the great legend. But that couldn't be farther from the truth.

The truth was, she was goddess damn *nervous* and without an outlet for her nerves, she told stories instead. Clearly, Remnant Dark was prominent on her mind. As it was for us both.

It had been six months since we fled the City of Light, six months we had been looking over our shoulders every minute of every day. Six months of Xi being convinced that we did not get away unnoticed and that it was only a matter of time before the shadow fae general came for us.

Hands waved in grand gestures as she spun her tale, I watched with the same enraptured attention as the rest of the poor bastards in the tavern. All of us fell for her allure, mesmerized by the sound of her voice and the way her hair swayed over lush lips, eager to catch just a glimpse of the hidden beauty beneath those silky white layers.

I wished she felt confident enough to show off her beauty. Her olive skin and stunning grey eyes, the color of the sky after calming from a storm, were a sight to behold, and right now they gleamed with such a teasing brightness, I felt myself grow hard just watching her.

But that was never anything new. When it came to my desire for her, it was never calm, always wanting, always needing. And if she did one day decide to unshield her face then that meant I would have to share her with others. Selfishly, I did not want that.

I had killed others for a lot less than looking at her. Besides, I liked the fact that I was the only one she trusted to see her true face, no matter how much of a curse she thought it was, no matter how much we occasionally took other lovers. Her true self was always mine to behold.

Grinning, I took another swig of my spiced ale when gasps ensued, the tension I had been feeling in my shoulders melting from my body only to increase *somewhere else*. Draping myself against the bar, I shifted from the increased tightness of my arousal and watched her with pride, feeling the eyes of others fall on me every so often as if asking my permission to admire her.

My grin grew. We were known as many things—lovers, friends, the elemental twins of the plains, but one thing we were always known for was being one. The times when we were not were now a long distant memory. Tied by our need to protect what we loved the most we had stayed together from the time of the Blood Wars till now. Passionate in our agenda to always support the fae of the elemental court.

That was our mission. Especially since Deirdre's rule seemed to steadily strip away their freedoms.

Licking my lips, I continued to enjoy the pleasant buzzing of the alcohol in my system. It was the most calm I had felt in weeks. Perhaps we truly had nothing to worry about.

"You better watch out Riley. Your girl is gaining enough attention that you may have to fend off some suitors."

Looking at the bartender, I gave him a wink, "You know we don't work that way Ura."

The fire elemental shook his head at me, nodding towards Xi, "I know it, and I tell you the same thing every time. Don't be a fucking goddess damn fool Riley Dragoon."

Tilting my head in his direction, I raised my glass to him, my green hair falling over my brow. "And don't be a goddess fucking buttinsky, Ura Purn."

He snickered, sliding a tray of liquid shots towards me. It was his newest concoction called Hydra's Piss. Meant to keep fae fucked up on a euphoric high that was not easily burned out of our system by our healing capabilities. It was what half this crowd was in here for aside from Xi's stories. "Make yourself of use, Dragoon, and pass these out to your girl's admirers. I want to see them pissed enough that they drop all their coins on my bar tonight. Between her storytelling and these drinks, it's sure to be a good night for me even if it won't be one for you. Your bed will be empty by the looks of it."

Laughing, I set my ale down, grabbing a shot for myself to shoot him a sardonic look. "You know I don't work here right?"

Ura arched a brow at me as I chugged the foul drink back, "And you know I never charge yeh or your female. Now be off."

Numbness flowed through my body, a steady warmth that spread from my stomach outwards, the Hydra Piss easing that last bit of tension pinching between my shoulder blades. Picking up the tray, I carried it over to the crowd that hovered around Xi.

Placing it on the table in front of them, Xi paused and looked up at me. Smirking, I slid a shot towards her. "You look parched."

She rolled her uncovered grey eye, but took the shot from my hand, my air whispering over her fingertips like I always did—enjoying the way her body shivered.

"On the house from Ura," I called out to the onlookers, who eagerly lunged for the drinks.

"Oi! Boy, push off, can't you see the lady is telling a story, she isn't interested in the likes of yeh!" shouted a crass sounding fae from the back of the room.

Xi laughed, setting down her shot without taking a sip.

I winked down at her, "Ouch, say it isn't true, Xi?"

She shook her head at me, white hair swaying over her shoulders, the sharp angled cut allowing her to cover her face easily.

"Come on bro, she is in the middle of the story and we want to know what will happen next," another complainer called out.

Xi grinned, blowing me a kiss, "The mob has spoken, Dragoon."

Planting my arms on the table I leaned into her space, loving the way her eye flickered down my body before stopping herself. Ura was a prick...there was no way my bed was going to be empty tonight. I had a feeling that it was going to be a lovers more than friends kind of night. I licked at my bottom lip watching her eyes darken with need. "I'll remember this later, earth baby."

She inhaled sharply. A sound only I could hear because it was the best sound air could make. Sexy and stilted. Oh yes, she would be mine tonight.

Pulling away, I flourished my hand, "By your leave, my lady."

Her uncovered grey eye flashed with annoyance and amusement.

"Finally!" someone breathed out. "Tell us what happened! How do you know her shadows command the dead?"

Xi turned back to them and she held up her hands, "Easy, easy. I was told so by the witch of the goddess plains. He said when they roam over the plains those that died on the fields are ripped up from their resting place, and then they hunt. But this time the shadows took on a new fight, the spirit realm, during the night of The Wailing."

I shivered. That was the worst night of my life. Samhain...when the veil between the spirit world and the real one thinned. During this time, the fae celebrated. We drank with lost souls, danced with loved ones, and fell into our deepest desires through the unlimited illusion of the spirit realm. Except that wasn't what happened when Xi and I had made the long pilgrimage to the sacred lands. What happened had been goddess damn carnage.

Instead of the veil thinning the worlds collided, melding into one, and the spirits took over—possessing thousands of fae gathering for revelry. With sterility plaguing our people, many had joined together for an excuse to celebrate life when we could no longer experience the joy of it ourselves through future progeny. But instead of drunken debauchery and sloppy seduction, there was blood and death. The spirit realm turned fae against fae, friends into foes, brethren into enemies.

I had almost lost Xi that night.

Shuddering, I studied the animated half of her face, and ignored the image of her soaked in blood, her throat sliced open from the end of a scythe and the damning choice I had made to save her.

She remembered only the final end of that day. Never knowing the way I had scooped her up in my arms, my hand slick with her blood, while I did the one thing I had never done before when danger came my way. I ran away. Away from the slaughter while I screamed, raged, and prayed to the deaf ears of the goddess to save her.

Except, that wasn't how life worked. Begging, pleading, and prayers did nothing for the fae of Faerie...especially for me. Sometimes one had to take fate into their own hands and tell destiny to fuck off, even if it meant using a dark forbidden power I once vowed to my parents to never ever use. Not for any circumstance.

When her beautiful grey eyes finally flashed open that night, I practically drowned in my own relief and guilt. Holding her tightly, we recovered and watched in eerie silence as darkness suddenly rolled in across the valley. It was quickly followed by wind, fire, and earth. Finally coming to our aide, walking side by side, the queen of Faerie, Deirdre Seelie and her shadow fae war general, Remnant Dark, faced the spirit realm without a flicker of fear or uncertainty.

That was the first time we had seen the infinite power of the shadows and realized one very important lesson. Remnant Dark's power far surpassed that of the queen of Faerie.

On cue, Xi's story picked up where my memories had led and I turned my attention back to her. "Together they walked through the blood soaked lands, silver and black, with all the elements forming a tidal wave of death that met the spirit realm with not even a single flicker of fear. Taking on the task of closing the spirit veil, the queen left General Dark's side for her to face hundreds of mad rabid fae on her own. Dancing across the plains, with her black sword whirling in the night, she cut down spirits without mercy. But it was her shadows, her loyal pets of the damned, that instilled fear into every surviving soul there. Their darkness latched onto the possessed fae and drained them slowly of all their life forces..." Leaning forward, she peered into the silent crowd, every single soul here, including myself, hanging onto her next words, "and you know what she said as they did it?"

Enamored and drunk on Hydra Piss, I didn't even notice that the tavern had gone quiet. The air was still as if collectively they all held their breath, fearful eyes no longer on Xi but directed beyond, towards the entrance.

I inhaled sharply when the darkness crept in waves from the open doorway and then snapped swiftly in a puff of smoke to the very table Xi sat at.

Fuck. Fuck. *Fuck.*

She was here. Remnant Dark, the general of Faerie's throne, the most powerful shadow fae alive was fucking here.

In the dead silence the chair across from Xi scraped harshly against the floor, pulled out by a lean, toned arm full of swirling tattooed ink. Wearing fitted black leather, Remnant Dark sat down gracefully. With her hair pulled back sharply in a ponytail that trailed over the back of the chair, the shadow fae general's famous green eyes were distinguished even more, highlighting the current bright light and mirth held within their emerald depths.

Xi met my eyes briefly in panic before her singular one stared back at the shadow fae sitting across from her. The darkness undulated in waves from the chair, forcing the fae around us to step backwards on whispered feet while I did the exact opposite.

Stepping into deadly shadows, I stood behind my friend. For if we were to face death, then we would sure as fuck do it together.

"Go on then," Remnant Dark said, tapping on the table with a single digit. Her voice was unlike anything I ever heard. Dark and commanding but also safe, alluring, like it had the power to change the world. "Finish the story, Xi Chin. What *exactly* did I say?"

CHAPTER 2

I STARED INTO THE very eyes that had been part of my waking nightmare for the past six months.

Her brow arched as she watched me stare like a goddess damn ninny. My words escaped me along with my soul that seemed to run as far from here as it possibly could, leaving my body to betray itself in the presence of a great power that some called monstrous.

Riley stepped closer, his strong presence bolstering the confidence I so desperately needed as shadows trailed around our feet, sniffing out our deceit like a bloodhound. My mouth opened but still no words came out.

"Can we help you, General Dark?" Riley said confidently over my head.

Tilting her head towards him, her long ponytail slid over her shoulder in blue black waves. "I am not entirely sure if that's the correct question to ask me, Riley Dragoon. I believe it is more or less if you are *willing* to help me, isn't it? But first I'd like to know the end of this lovely story." Looking back at me, her emerald green eyes seized my heart, skittering its thunderous beat to a full stop before accelerating faster than before.

Panic set in. She *knew.* She had to know.

Riley's wind fluttered against the back of my neck, stirring my hair, and calming my racing pulse. I exhaled slowly, licking at my suddenly chapped lips then narrowing my gaze, chin lifted. I would not fear her. Only victims feared others and I would never be a victim again. "You said spirits make the shadows go tipsy because they are light on the palette."

It seemed like the world slowed down with the blink of her eyes and then sped back up again when she released a loud snicker, leaning back in her chair to cross her powerful legs. Her booted foot bounced with thought, "Well I suppose that is better than the last version I heard of The Wailing."

I licked at my lips again. "You said you would see if we are willing to help you. Now I want to know with what exactly? How can the humble fae of the plains *willfully* help the general of Faerie?"

Clinging to the slow bounce of her foot, the shadows crawled along it, already bored with their perusal and needing some sort of new stimulus to occupy them while mother had a chat with friends. Except we were not her friends and if she knew what we had done, chances were we were now her direct enemy.

"Of course," she said, her eyes flashing, "I suppose this information is for all here to hear." Briefly her gaze fell on the crowd of fae giving her a wide berth, shifting away the moment her eyes trailed off of them in her scrutiny. Faces pale, eyes wide, they couldn't look away from her even though they wanted to run. Her eyes settled back to me, nodding softly to herself. "It has come to the Capital's attention that something was stolen from the palace on the night of the Winter Solstice. An artifact to be precise. An artifact that I have tracked to these plains. Unfortunately, the trail has gone somewhat *awry.*"

My stomach sank and my hair fell in a soft curtain across my face but I did not react. Staying still. "And what exactly is this artifact you speak of?"

The shadows tick-tocked lazily with her boot, slow deadly pendulums of darkness. "One half of twin seals, shaped as a small disc, made of molten rock from the bowels of Hell. Without its twin, this seal will bring wrath down upon Faerie."

Molten rock? That sounded a lot like firestone to me. I caught Riley's eye briefly before smoothing over any other reactions I may have revealed.

"We have no knowledge of a seal," I replied confidently, refusing to acknowledge the coincidence of a *sacred* seal going missing the same time we took something else...something far more precious.

Her lips pressed into a thin line while she uncrossed her legs, feet hitting the floor in a soft thud to sit straighter in her chair. An action that ensnared us all in her powerful and alluring scrutiny. "I wouldn't expect you to...however, I am in need of two fae that know these parts well enough and have the skill set I require to assist me in tracking it down. I've been told you both served under Lord Oberon in the Blood Wars. Am I wrong?"

I glanced up at Riley, folding his arms across his chest, a sneer pulled across his handsome face, "You mean when we served under him for about a month before his untimely death in the wars? I'm sure you know of that particular story, don't you, general? It was the queen after all who was the only one to survive the slaughter. I'm sure she told you all about it."

Utter silence, not a single fae breathed.

Skipping licking my lips this time, I bit them instead, my nerves fully charged. We were going to die here. There was no way around it. I'd seen her take out fae for much less.

Raising her brows, the shadow fae general shook her head, "I prefer to do my own research, Riley Dragoon and my research tells me the two of you are exactly who I need," Rising, she snuffed the shadows out with her hand and despite her short stature, she was still a living breathing goddess amongst us. Untouchable in our reality.

"Then your resources were fucked, general," I snorted for the first time, rolling my eyes without realizing what I was doing. Riley's air immediately rushed around me protectively, while another round of sharp collective inhales sucked out the rest in the room.

She smiled down at me, knowing glittering in her eyes, "No, I don't think they were, actually." Shadows flowed down from her arm and I was thankful for the high back chair or else she would have seen me recoil from their dark tendril abyss. Eyes wide, I watched as they picked up my full Hydra Piss shot and placed it gracefully in her hand, not a single drop spilled. Throwing it back without taking her eyes off of mine, she discarded it rim-side down.

The sound echoed throughout the room making those around us flinch while there was not even a single twitch in her body from the drink I knew tasted like acidic poison. "But I will tell you this. It would be prudent for you to join me, there are fates worse than The Wailing, worse than even the loss of your people from a queen you despise, and I cannot guarantee my protection should that time come."

I swallowed hard. My relief in believing she knew nothing of what we stole ripped from me. Riley and I's goal had been to always keep the elemental court safe and free of Deirdre's clutches—and what she was alluding to tonight, was that whatever power this seal had...our people would not survive it.

And it seemed neither would we, why else would we need her protection? She was our enemy, wasn't she?

Shrugging, she winked, "I'll give you until morning to decide, after that I can linger no longer but the choice will still be yours." Turning to Ura who stood stoically behind the tavern's bar, she added lightly, "I don't suppose you have any rooms available in your fine establishment?"

Ura glanced back at Riley and me before crossing his arms in front of his chest with false bravado, "Nay, General Dark, there are no available rooms for you here."

I withheld a groan. I knew for a fact that Ura had more than a few rooms available. There were so few of us out on the goddess plains now, and Remnant Dark would know that too.

She nodded politely, "Funny thing that. The last two taverns I visited had the same response. However, I suspect there *is* a room available for a fae who is not the general to the throne."

Ura stiffened and I held my breath, the fool.

She snickered, "Worry not bartender, a monster like me belongs uncaged under the stars and not in the confining bars of fake civility." Waving her shadows, a large bag thumped onto the bar, coins spilling out in a loud clatter on the smooth polished wood. "For your trouble, I am sure my presence has cost you some revenue this night."

Ura stared at the pile of gold as did the rest of us. Slowly, he looked back up at her, "I need none of the queen's gold here, General. We will be just fine without her generosity."

Flipping her long ponytail back over her shoulder she gave him a knowing look, "Well then it's a good thing that this isn't the queen's coin, Ura Ohnz. Never forget I was the daughter of the Lady of Night first, Princess of the Shadows." Looking at the hovering darkness, she added, "Come my loves, we are no longer welcome here." Spinning, she gave us both one more wink before walking out the door, her shadows trailing behind her like smoke blowing in the breeze.

I counted to ten. Ten seconds of holding my breath after the door had closed with a sharp click. "Goddess," I whispered on a harsh exhale as the tavern's gossip roared anew with terrified excitement.

"I wouldn't pray to her, Xi. She abandoned us a long time ago and she isn't going to help us out of this Faerie shit," Riley hummed darkly, a strained edge to his tone. I glanced up, seeing more than a few ghosts of haunted memories in his eyes.

CHAPTER 3

I STARED UP AT the enchanted ceiling meant to mimic the stars outside. Most elemental fae preferred the solace of the outdoors, being one with the environment that we manipulated daily. So it was no surprise that each one of these rooms were spelled to resonate just that.

The irony of it all was that the shadow fae general, denied a room here, was enjoying the real comforts of the elements right now. Staring up at real stars instead of enchanted ones, and I couldn't help but wonder what she thought when they sparkled down upon her.

Frowning, I laced my hands behind my head. While the General *was* terrifying, there was something so purely honest and determined in her expression. As if she were fighting a war on a scale none of us could even fathom—all alone.

And for that, a part of me felt compelled to kneel before her and pledge my services, a pull that foretold my destiny like it was written in the stars she was sleeping under. Gritting my teeth, I fought that urge even now, for there was only one fae in this world that had ever made me feel that way and she was currently fucking someone else in the room down the hall.

The moment the General appeared, I knew Xi would no longer be seeking my bed as I had hoped for previously. I was a goddess damn reminder of the decision we would need to make soon—join and play along, or run and likely watch our entire court die. My teeth ground harder thinking of someone else in her arms. Kissing her, touching her. In the past, this would have never bothered me, having done the same myself plenty of times before—except right now I needed her to sort through this epic shit we found ourselves in.

That's the verity I clung to anyway, because the other half was something that I could not acknowledge. I sealed our fate the moment I saved her all those years ago. It was *wrong* of me to want her, wrong for me to want to possess every part of her because in truth, I already did.

I owned Xi Chin.

But not in the breathtaking way of soulmates because, of course, that would have been too much of a fucking ask from this world. No. It was the exact opposite of that, a monstrous thing that if even allowed a whisper of my attention, I feared would be unleashed to destroy everything I had...and that breathtaking dream I wished for.

Sighing, I shook my head to rid myself of the dark self-loathing path I was treading on and trailed one hand from the back of my head down the front of my naked body. Grabbing my cock, I slowly pumped it. Hardening instantly, blue balled since Remnant Dark stormed in, my cock was eager for release.

Perhaps this was the cause of my perseverating thoughts...perhaps a release from this pent up tension was exactly what I needed to solve the distinct feeling that Xi and I were fucked five ways to Sheol and back, with my own soul marked for the death god himself.

I groaned as my hand quickened, my shaft growing even harder under my firm grasp. Closing my eyes, I conjured up the last time I sunk my cock into Xi's warm depths. It was on the night of the solstice when we were high on the euphoria of accomplishing our task and also terrified of the consequences if we got caught.

The adrenaline sparking a feral passion that only we knew how to satisfy within one another.

My hand hastened and my thighs clenched, hips meeting my fierce downward stroke, my elemental power whispered around me, mimicking the hot breath that was the memory of Xi's gasps.

Another groan, I was close—.

"Ri, you asleep?" I stilled at the sound of Xi's voice beyond the door, rapping on it urgently.

Eyes snapping open I inhaled deeply, releasing my throbbing cock with a stifled groan, I rose from the bed, shucking on my leathers I had casually discarded on the floor. Stumbling when another loud rapping made me fumble with the damned ties. "Fuck it already," I muttered when the door banged again, the laces would just have to stay...undone. "Yea I'm up, hang on," I called out huskily.

Walking on bare feet across the marble surface, my pants swinging dangerously low off my hips, I threw open the door to see the object of my sexual fantasies leaning against the doorframe, a smug smile on her face and two shot glasses with a bottle of Hydra Piss in hand.

Her tongue snaked out, licking her lips as she caught the full sight of me. Her gaze a whisper of sweet desire as it fell downward over my naked chest, and lower still, where my pants hung open, and my dick stood proudly flushed against my toned stomach. Her eyes lingered there for a moment before sweeping outward, following the wings of the tattooed phoenix branded across my pelvis, its feathered tips wrapping all the way to the back of my ass. Artwork that she loved to trace with her tongue. Even now, it swept across her parched lips staring hungrily at the mark of my rebellious homage to the great bird that commanded the vast air currents of Faerie's skies—skies I now controlled after crawling out from my own rebirth.

Following my ink back inward, Xi's gaze fell on the vicious bowed head of the phoenix covering my groin, submitting to my now bulging erection. I couldn't help but smirk, satisfied at the way her breathing became more shallow, her uncovered eye dilating with passion.

Either the poor schmuck she had taken to her bed came in his pants right when she touched him or her night didn't go exactly how she expected because her clothing was tidy, her hair still smooth when it should be a disheveled mess, her face revealed to expose the magnificent beauty of a female well fucked.

"What can I do for you my terrella?" *Little earth.* I had been calling her that since we first met in the dark tunnels of the underground I had been lost in.

"Can I stay with you tonight?" she purred and I could smell the slight tinge of alcohol on her breath. Holding up the shot glasses and spirits, smiling at the way I was caught staring at her, she quirked her brow. "Well?"

Plucking the Hydra Piss from her hand, I stepped aside, popping the cork. "How could I ever deny you, when you bear such poisonous gifts?"

She snickered and padded inside, looking around my room suspiciously. "You weren't entertaining were you?"

Quietly shutting the door with my wind and throwing the lock, I took a large swig of the potent alcohol straight from the bottle. If I wasn't going to get off, then letting the alcohol numb my body like before seemed to be the next best thing.

"I wasn't in the mood," I said, sending my breeze across the room to unveil the beautiful face that still stole my fucking air everytime I looked upon it. Walking around her, I took another long drink, enjoying the foul burn, "What of you, did your bed partner disappoint?"

"I sent him down to the sweet little fae who was batting her lashes at him all night."

She reached for the bottle but I tsked, holding one finger up and cocking it side to side. She scowled back, and I watched amused and enthralled by the way her perfect features wrinkled adorably on her face. My cock growing harder at the sight. "You've had plenty and I haven't had nearly enough."

Laughing at her darkening look, I grabbed her hand and brought her to the center of the room. Grabbing two pillows from the nearby chairs I threw them on the floor. Xi didn't like chairs, she preferred to be close to the earth as often as possible. In this case, the marble would have to do but that did not mean I wanted to sit rigidly on the cold ass floor.

Guiding her to the pillows, I twirled her before allowing my air to softly wrap around her perfect curves, slowly lowering her down to the cushion like a proper high lady of the elemental court.

Joining her, I felt her grey eyes drop to my open pants again, and I preened with male pride inside. Even if she had chose another lover tonight, she was still here, eye fucking me like she should have been hours before this. Leaning forward, I set the bottle down between us and plucked the shot glasses from her hands, placing one on either side of the bottle.

"For old times sake, back when we served. Shot for shot. Question for question." I arched a brow at her. "Let us think this through." Lifting the bottle with my air, I filled our glasses and then gave her a knowing look. "Ask."

"Do you think she knows what we stole?" Xi asked in a squeaky rush and it was the cutest sound I had ever heard.

Grabbing my glass I threw it back, letting it add to the buzz that was already a pleasant burn through my system. Licking my lips, her eyes dilated more, I spoke slowly, "I think that when it comes to General Remnant Dark it is safe to assume she knows all." Leaning back on my hands, I stared into her passion-blown eyes. "The real question is, do you want to join her on the search for the seal?"

Reaching for the shot glass she took the spirits in one swallow and goddess damn it, it was fucking sexy as Sheol. I wanted nothing more than to feel her hot mouth swallowing down my brutal erection still throbbing, barely restrained by my loose pants. "Do we have a fucking choice?" she finally replied.

Guiding the air to pour us another round, I sighed, drinking my shot before tilting my head back to frown at the enchanted ceiling. "There is always a choice Xi. Either we run forever to escape certain death and risk the lives of our people or we play her game with an unknown end...and her *protection*?"

Scowling, she glared at me. "How could she protect us Ri? She is our enemy! Pledged to her queen, her lover for goddess sakes!"

The fake stars shimmered. "Perhaps that is what we are made to think...perhaps she is playing a game that we are not aware of, where the *queen* is her enemy."

"Don't be ridiculous, Ri," she snapped and I shrugged.

How else could I explain my own draw towards the lethal shadow fae, surely I would not align myself with a creature that was evil...but a fae misunderstood? That—that I could understand.

The silence stretched between us before Xi sighed again, tugging on her hair and resisting the urge to pull it back across her face to hide. "I take it you are in favor of joining her then?"

Smirking, still watching the ceiling, I heard her gasp when I let the air flow over her body, tilting her own head back.

"Do you want more?" I asked silkily, bringing my gaze back to watch the show as the shot rose in front of her, brushing against her lips. Her mouth parting in the most sensual sigh.

"Yes," she whispered.

My cock jumped at the sound and her consent. Fucking goddess. She was my match in every way.

"Then drink," I purred, watching as I pressed the glass against her lips and slowly poured it into her mouth, pausing to allow her to swallow, lick, and begin again. Ounce by ounce.

Sweet fucking goddess.

Pulling the glass away, I released her head from my power and watched as she brought those gorgeous stormy eyes back to mine.

"What is it you want to do, terrella?" I choked, my self control waning.

Licking her lips, her small tits rising and falling with her aroused breathing, she studied me carefully before whispering huskily, "Play."

My brows raised as I unfurled my legs, watching her eyes drop again. "I beg your pardon, Xi, what kind of play are we talking about? The General's or ours."

Her gaze snapped to mine and I felt my heart seize briefly. Goddess, why did her eyes remind me so much of air? Air I could bend to my will any day but never could I sway hers. "Both, Ri. I want to play both."

I groaned, "Then come to me, my terrella, and show me exactly how you want to play."

Her eyes blazed, and she bit at her plump bottom lip before leaning forward, brushing the bottle aside and slowly crawling across the floor.

Fuck me. Yes. I wanted her to fuck me. I watched her sensual movement through hooded eyes and with bated breath, my fingers digging into the marble when she climbed up on my lap, her legs straddling my own. Hands reaching down to slowly spread wide over my abdomen, my breath caught, fingertips tracing the large wings tattooed across my pelvis before plunging into my pants, gripping my throbbing dick fiercely.

"Shit, fuck," I barked, her strong steady hand pulling my cock further from my pants, revealing more dark ink of thick black bands. Pumping, her fingers trailed over the sensitive markings, setting a slow rhythm that was nothing short of sinful agony.

"Would you cum for me like this Ri?" her breath whispered across my lips, her thumb swiping over my cockhead, gathering my precum and using it to enhance her pumping hand.

Flashbacks of the times when we huddled in camps together, bed rolls close, her hand slipping between us, swallowing down our gasps with devouring kisses while everyone else slept nearby came to mind. I smirked up at the ceiling, there was never any doubt I would always cum for her in any way she delivered it to me.

Closing the space between us, I rose, my mouth slamming into hers, my hands sliding up her torso, thumbs brushing over the taut fabric of her shirt where her hardened nipples pebbled through, I groaned, "You know I will terrella."

Her hand squeezed harder and her pace quickened, drawing a loud hiss from me and the immediate desire to retaliate. Plunging my power down into her skin-tight pants, I whispered it over her clit, and grinned at her surprised gasps.

"Ri, that's, oh—." Her mouth pulled away from mine when I plunged my power deep into her pussy, knowing it was slick with her desire. I could fucking smell it on the air, practically taste it with each stirring breath. Her white hair fell even further away from her face when she moaned up at the enchanted ceiling, "That's cheating, Dragoon."

I chuckled.

Frantically, she pumped me harder, and I thrusted into her hand with loud moaning grunts watching the rapture on her gorgeous face. Returning the favor, I shoved my air deeper, pulsating the element in the exact way she loved.

"That's it my little earth baby, fucking ride my power, feel it deep inside you, you know only I can make you feel this good and I am not even inside you yet," I snarled, kissing up her throat, sending more of my power washing over her body, caressing and whispering over her skin beneath her clothes with a thousand sacred kisses of soft cool air.

"Yes," she gasped, losing herself in the feel of me and only me.

I was fucking close, her hand pumping me just right, her thrusting hips adding even more to the sensual torture but I wasn't about to cum before Xi did. Moaning with her, I guided my air to trickle further between her legs up to her perfect little rosebud. Rimming it with my power.

Xi screamed, her body thrusting into me wildly, jerking my cock with a savage rhythm that sent me completely over the fucking edge.

Roaring against her throat I came, pulling her tightly into me, my body shuddering with the violent release, my dick spasming hot cum between us, coating our clothing. All the while, I felt her tight pussy do the same on the power I slowly eased from her body.

Aside from our heavy breathing, the room was silent once more and when her head lowered back down to me, I was caught by the love I saw in her eyes.

Love we had never spoken of, in fact we blatantly ignored it, satisfied with how our relationship was...but goddess damn it, in this moment, I would have reverently bowed down on my knees to beg her for something so much more. But she wasn't ready yet, she likely never would be.

Weaving the air, I poured the shot glasses behind her back and lifted them to float between us, knowing our activities had burned most of the alcohol from our system. Hydra Piss was good, better than most spirits, but when it came to the fae we were always superior.

A slow smile spread across her face. "Round two?" She quirked a brow, plucking the glass from the air.

I grinned back, knowing she meant that in more ways than one. Fuck, I was one lucky bastard of a fae. "Yes, my terrella. Round two. You still have clothes on after all."

CHAPTER 4

Remnant

I BLINKED SLOWLY AT the mess, hardly believing only two fae were involved in what looked like an unhinged orgy. Clothes were strewn all over, several bottles of the strong spirits I sampled last night littered the floor, and amongst them were two very naked fae reeking of sex and bathed in cum. A bare white ass greeted me with a tattoo peek of feathered wings cradling each sculpted cheek wrapping to the front—my brows rose, more than curious to see the rest.

Leaning back on the windowsill, praying that at least this spot had come out unscathed from the events of last night, I quirked a brow and cleared my throat, "I'm wondering if I should take offense for not being invited to this party?"

A green head of hair shot up accompanied by a rush of air. Flicking my hand with shadows, they swallowed the dangerous air power just in time to reveal a very startled, very handsome, and very naked air elemental. My gaze trailed amusedly over his lean-cut frame, noticing the brands on his skin actually did spread fully across his groin. A phoenix in mid-flight to be exact, its wings spread for attack, the ink following even further across his shaft.

Smirking, I lifted my ogling stare to meet his slightly panicked, and yet even more smug expression. Pressing my lips into a thin line, I suppressed my laughter when his foot kicked out, quickly nudging this partner still sleeping soundly on the floor.

"Fuck Ri, is that your foot, stop kicking me." The other elemental, Xi Chin, murmured still half asleep, her white hair caked across her face.

Hazel eyes never left mine, his stance solid, no shame in his exposure, and ready to fight me if he must. "General Dark, apologies for just now. I hadn't realized it was you," he said, kicking Xi more frantically this time.

"Xi, General Dark is here. Now. As in the veritable flesh."

"Stop goddess damn kicking me, and that's not even fucking funny, Ri," she groaned back, then snickered. "But if she were here I'd tell her to piss off, shove her shadows where the sun doesn't shine, and never show her face here again."

My grin widened at the comical look that spread across the air elemental's face. A cross between choking horror and grim determination. "Am I to believe that's your final answer then, Xi Chin, in regards to joining me in search of the seal that is?"

The snickering earth elemental stilled, suddenly quiet she quickly pushed to standing. Her grey eyes widened just before she bowed low in all her naked glory, "General Dark, fuck. Apologies, I—"

I held up my hand. "I am not a morning person either nor would I be after," my eyes trailed across the room but I did not miss the way they both flinched when I did so, "after whatever this goddess damn was." Flicking my long hair back over my shoulder, I returned to studying them, gathering the shadows behind me. "I tell you what. To make it up to me, I could use some company for breakfast. The tavern's cook seems much more accommodating than any others I have come across and she has agreed to prepare us all a spread." The shadows plumed up around my feet, absorbing me into their darkness, to shift through the void. A trick of the eye that was useful but limited in distance. I sighed inwardly, thinking for the millionth time in my life how much simpler it would be if they could actually teleport. A fae could dream I suppose. Winking back at their stunned faces, I continued, "See you downstairs, we can talk more then."

As I shifted through the hidden shadows, Xi's whisper did not escape me, "I don't like this, why is it when-ever she speaks I feel this intense foreboding and the winking...that just makes it worse."

I smiled, moving further away then stepping out of the shadows into a small corner of the room below where we would be away from prying eyes and eavesdroppers. Being the only shadow fae in these parts drew much attention—mostly bad. Being the only shadow fae *and* war general to the throne made it so much worse.

But this was the life I chose, aligning myself with the queen. What I hadn't anticipated was us becoming lovers, or the joy we found in being one of the two loneliest beings in this world. Perhaps there was a part of me that believed I could be the one to make her find another way, guide her towards helping our people and steering her away from the power-hungry madness simmering below the surface.

But I had been wrong and now I had no one to trust but me and my shadows. Being here today gave me hope that perhaps it wouldn't always be that way.

A large-bodied shadow loomed over me where I sat. I had felt him approach, despite being lost in memories, expecting the uncordial greeting.

"I think it's best you be on your way, shadow fae." A gravelly voice above just held back the tremble in their tone.

Leaning back in the booth, I tilted my head to the side. He was a tall fae, with chestnut hair and eyes of auburn that scorched the air between us. It took a lot to confront the General of Faerie even if he did have a strong athletic frame. A formidable opponent aside from needing a few good meals and perhaps clothing that was not so threadbare. The fae of these plains were suffering, that much was clear, "Good morning, what is your name?"

"Did you hear what I said?" he growled, slapping his hands on the table.

I waved my own, the shadows swirling around it. *Show offs.* "Let me take a guess, fire elemental?"

He scowled, leaning into my space. I didn't like fae in my space but I also didn't like seeing the fear flickering in his eyes despite his bravado. This wasn't a truly aggressive fae, it was one who was terrified and worried for the people he loved here.

But I was and never had been a fae that could be controlled nor commanded. A fact that drove the queen into fits of rage. She loved me for my power and what it could do. Power I would never allow her to have, the first splinter in our relationship.

Sighing, I released the shadows. "Tell you what, I'll challenge you to a contest." Throwing a silver blade from my boot into the table between his hands, I smiled at his widened eyes. "Dodging daggers. If you can hit me, then I'll leave."

The fire elemental's lips thinned, looking between me and the dagger. Admittedly, I was surprised he was still standing here, that fact alone took balls and I *liked* it. Staring at the blade momentarily, calculating his options, he released a low growl, "Without your powers? And if I win, you leave and never come back here? No questions asked?"

I hummed, "Yes, and I'll even wear the blindfold. Deal?"

His auburn eyes gleamed and his tongue licked across his teeth. "Deal."

Rising from the booth, I wrenched the dagger out of the wooden table, handing it over to him, and manifesting a thick strip of cloth from my shadow void. I was most fortunate to have the shadows carry everything for me while traveling and of course, one could never travel anywhere without daggers and blindfolds. "Goddess' blessings to you then, fire elemental."

Wrapping the blindfold around my head, I picked my way through the tavern full of chairs and barstools, having already memorized the space in my mind. Turning at the appropriate amount of paces.

"Ten second countdown," I cooed, "Ten...nine...eight...seven...six...five...four...three..." A slight shift, a soft whirl, and I spun, dancing to the side, hearing the loud thunk of the blade hitting the wall instead of my body.

A loud curse echoed throughout the room while I unshielded myself from the blindfold only to see fire shooting towards my head. I was ready for it, of course I was, I had already sensed scorching eyes was a sore loser, short tempered but most of all, afraid. Fear made fae do foolish things.

Quickly, I snuffed it out, the shadows hissing. Not enjoying the light they were forced to consume.

"Bad form, Caval. You made a deal with the general, you should honor it!"

Turning, I watched a freshly showered Riley Dragoon stroll forward with his partner Xi following stride for stride, her lips pressed harshly together with disapproval. I cocked my head, wondering if they realized how in sync they were with each other. Air and earth, an unlikely pair, and yet the way they moved, their presence, and bond was the most natural thing I had ever seen.

Part of me ached for a bond like that but that seemed very unlikely. The time of soulmates was far and few, with the slow extinction of our race, there were no new souls to be born. Our curse of infertility set up our impending extinction but also stopped the natural course of fate. A demise that was slow—allowing a long life but not a full one.

That was if we didn't kill each other off first.

The fire elemental's mouth opened and closed, his eyes wide with fright. "I...I, please forgive—I don't know what came over me."

I shook my head, "You have a decent throw, *Caval*," I said, walking towards the wall and grabbing the dagger. "I could use someone like you to join my forces, I am always looking for elementals who can see past their fear to protect the fae they love. You just need a bit more training to truly harness it."

The squeak of the cook stepping into the room had us all looking in her direction. Face blushing deep red, she scurried to the table to drop off a loaded tray of delicious looking fare, and then dashed back out of the room. All of us followed her retreat before turning back to one another.

Smirking, I tossed a silver coin to Caval. His demeanor now one of shock as he flipped it over in the palm of his hand, "If you're interested, take that to the guards at the gates of the City of Light, show them the coin and they will take you to Lieutenant Ruane. He will get you sorted, supplying you with anything you need. Including a full year's pay."

Both Xi and Riley inhaled sharply while the fire elemental stared at the coin in his hand. *Purpose*, Caval just needed a purpose for this life, and this was the first time he was realizing it.

Striding back towards the table of delicious smelling egg custard tarts and steamed buns with strawberry sauce I had ordered, I winked back at the fire elemental, "I'd get out of here Caval, before I change my mind."

Not bothering to look back, I heard Caval release a faint curse before whispering his goodbyes and apologies to the other two elementals in the room.

Sitting down, I smoothed out my fitted leather vest and used the dagger to distribute the tarts and buns on my plate, slathering them in a massacre of sweet, sticky strawberry sauce. Stabbing a tart with the blade, I stuffed the whole thing in my mouth looking up at the two elemental fae watching me warily. Chewing thoughtfully, I studied them. They weren't afraid or nervous as much as they were worried...and their worry was not for themselves. "So..." I said through a mouthful of custard, "about the item you actually *did* steal. The Empedolces staff."

CHAPTER 5

E MPEDOLCES STAFF.

The words echoed on repeat, clattering around in my brain along with my terror that I refused to show. We had worked too long and too hard to return what was once our court's most sacred treasure.

Clipped from the roots of the ancient grove by the goddess, the Empedolces was made of the four elemental sources of power. Fire, air, earth, and spirit, combined together into an enchanted wood. A staff that crowned the leader of the elemental court.

The last leader chosen by the staff was Oberon Adranos Unseelie, a powerful earth and fire elemental that fell in battle during the Blood Wars. His loss resonated throughout our people. We mourned, we grieved, and then *she* took the throne. Deirdre Tatianna Maeve Seelie, another powerful elemental that wielded all four elements, never chosen by the Empedolces, and yet still took over the rule. While our war-torn world accepted her as queen, the elementals were not so keen. Split between the ways of old and the queen's bright future promises, our people were on the brink of civil war.

We could no longer stay divided. The fracturing weakened everything that made the elemental court formidable, strong, and thriving. It was time our people were reunited again, under the true leader of our court and not the fake impersonation on the throne. Power wasn't always the markings of a great leader and Deirdre Seelie was anything but—she was an *opportunist.*

"The staff has not been seen by our people since the Blood Wars," I said with more courage than I felt inside.

"Oh that I very much believe, please sit." Remnant Dark waved to the seat next to her.

Riley grunted, sliding fluidly into the booth, snatching up a plate to pile it high with warm buns and sticky strawberry sauce. The shadow fae general watched him with an amused expression, stuffing another pastry tart in her mouth.

Catching my look, Riley snorted at me. "I am not about to pass up steamed buns, Xi." He winked at me salaciously and I blinked. The image of his own steamed buns in the shower just moments ago still vivid in my mind.

The general snickered and then raised an expectant brow at me.

"For fucks sake," I muttered, tugging on my bright white hair before sliding into a seat next to Riley.

Picking up a cup of hot tea, the shadow fae watched me from across the table, blowing delicately on the brew before taking a deep gratifying sip, sighing softly into her cup. The scent of mint and jasmine wafted out from the steam, and was soothing, despite my discomfort. "The queen does not know, she is more worried about the seal that has been stolen," she frowned and then shook her head, setting the cup down, "and I have no intention of telling her what you have done."

Both Riley and I stilled before I blurted out, "Why the fuck not?"

Riley's fork clattered on his plate and I winced, knowing then that I had made a huge mistake. I may as well have hanged myself on the city gates.

The shadow fae's emerald eyes gleamed like a predator getting closer to capturing her prey and fantasizing about all the ways she would enjoy her new prize.

"Shit," I whispered, my power flaring beneath us. I could split this room in half and sink her into the unforgiving earth while we made a break for our lives.

Reaching for me beneath the table, Riley's warm hand settled on my upper thigh to soothe me, his air whispering softly and quietly against my ear, "Wait, terrella."

Remnant smiled knowingly, "Be at ease, Xi Chin. I am not here due to your fine thievery, I am here to ask for your assistance in finding the seal. In return, I will give you the *real* Empedolces."

Riley and I both quickly glanced at each other. "What do you mean the *real* Empedolces?"

The General sliced into her steamed bun, at this point more sauce than dough. "Just that. The one you stole is a replica. I had it made the first night I noticed you at the Winter Solstice five years ago. Why else would an unknown elemental be there?"

Riley chewed his own food thoughtfully, the sound loud while I stared at the shadow fae in front of us with disbelief. The absolute absurdity that he was eating was beyond my comprehension. My stomach was currently tied in knots.

"How?" I whispered, the color draining from my face. We had been so careful, so tactical...

Her lips twitched, "Those are my secrets which you have yet to earn, Xi Chin." Leaning forward she tapped her finger on the table. "Here's the bargain. I will give you the real staff after you have given me your full assistance in tracking down the stolen seal."

"What is so special about this seal?" I snapped, surely it was not as important as the Empedocles. The one thing that could truly bring our shattered court back together.

Raising her finger, she counted off. "One, the queen is fully aware that it is gone and is ready to burn down every inch of this world to have it back in her possession. Two, it is the key to unlocking the gateway to the realm of Hell. And three, it has a twin that holds back the beasts of origin."

"You're serious," Riley narrowed his eyes, swallowing hard, "As in the fabled monsters the goddess created before the fae?"

She hummed, slicing another bun and bringing it to her lips, "Yep! And without its twin, the prison that holds them will weaken. I fear it already has." As if she had just told us the day was pleasant because the sun was shining, she popped the bun in her mouth, savoring her bite.

I bit on the inside of my cheek, well fuck, that *did* sound slightly more important than naming our next leader to take down the queen...we needed our people alive in order to do that. If the beasts of origin roamed our lands then they were at even more risk than before.

Riley crossed his arms, "None of this explains exactly why you chose us."

Eyes gleaming, she sipped her tea and I couldn't help but squirm under that omniscient stare. "Because you have something to lose, and everything to gain by helping me."

I narrowed my eyes on her, there was something she still wasn't telling us, wording her answers with a clever fae tongue.

Riley barked with laughter, "I call Faerie shit. You have been tracking the seal for six months and you can't find it. You do not have the upper hand here. You're equally as desperate as we are."

I stilled, my eyes widening. This time it wasn't my mouth that landed us in a fiery pit of Sheol, nay this time it was Riley's.

CHAPTER 6

THE GENERAL LAUGHED AND I stared at the vision she made.

Shadows of darkness swirled, her eyes glittered with the pure smile that lit them from within, and the sound of her voice was a sweet twilight symphony. An air fae could hear the song of the soul when a fae laughed and Remnant Dark's was the purest one I had ever heard. It spoke of kindred spirits, of fate intertwining, and somehow—it melted my fear of her.

All I saw here and now, was a young fae battling giants alone and it tugged at my heart. The strange urge I had last night called to me again telling me that I could trust this fae with every dark secret, show her every hidden scar, and place my life in her hands to keep safe forever.

It was different than the soul-crushing need and heart-seizing ache Xi stirred within me.

When her laughter trailed off a smirk stayed on her lips, her lethal fingers tapping gently on the delicate teacup. "Desperate? Perhaps I am but it is not for the reasons you are thinking."

I narrowed my eyes on her and crossed my arms over my chest. "I doubt even you know what I am thinking, General Dark." But there was still that small reluctant thought, that doubt that perhaps she could read everything in my soul.

She arched her brow, humming, "Maybe when this is all over you can determine that for yourself."

I stiffened. What the ever living fae fuck did that mean?

Leaning back against the booth, Remnant Dark's keen stare watched us both, the shadows settling in her lap in crumbling layers, a blanket of darkness. Timid like a kitten, it was an illusion of their monstrous abilities.

Xi shifted uncomfortably next to me and so did I. There was something wholly unhinged about her lethal shadows acting like a tenderhearted pet. I glanced towards Xi, her one uncovered eye already regarding me. One look, a thousand words. This was how it had always been between us and I knew her answer, just like I had known mine.

My mouth opened to give it to the waiting general but a sharp cry stopped me short and in a flash of shadow the general was gone, leaving behind an empty seat.

More screams joined the first and I realized that they were screams of terror, coming from outside.

Xi and I stood immediately with alarm. "Great," she spat, "of course something would happen now. Six months, six months of nothing, not a single sign of unrest and now the moment she comes here..."

Grabbing her arm I pulled her along with me, our strides falling harmoniously together, an easy feat as we were equals in height. "You hate everything you're not prepared for Xi, let's check out what all the commotion is."

"I'll tell you what it is, Riley Dragoon," she said, flinging her free hand wildly as we stepped through the doorway. "It's fucking trouble and now is our chance to make a goddess damn break for it. Instead we are heading straight into the thick of it!"

Ignoring her, I stepped into the quaint street lined with white flowers and soft moss. Blinking against the bright sun, I grabbed a gentle earth fae rushing by me amongst a sea of others, her face full of terror, her body shaking. "Juni, what is it?"

Wild light green eyes, so pale they were almost white darted back behind me. "They have come! The queen's forces have come to Croi! They have already started burning down the town." She tugged on her arm and I released her quickly, seeing the utter fear behind her eyes. "Please, I must go!" With a flourish of silk finery she twirled away from me without even awaiting my response.

"Why the fuck is no one trying to stop them?" I growled low, turning to see smoke in the cobalt skies of Faerie, my teeth grinding at the sight. The air stirred and I used it to thrust a path through the terrified mob, setting a running pace down the moss lined street with Xi keeping pace easily at my side.

"You know why Riley. They are terrified with what happened last time a town resisted," she hissed as we ran. "They are still hanging on the city walls."

I grunted, the image of their lifeless bodies still clear in my mind. "We are fucking elementals. We are what make this world balanced."

Xi yanked her hair over her face, her other arm swinging with her long running stride. "*They* are elementals too Ri...the most powerful ones, recruited by Her Majesty and..."

I gave her a sharp look, pushing our speed. "You think Remnant Dark brought them here."

She pursed her lips, her eyes narrowing at the thickened smoke. "Part of me does or wants to. It's hard to believe she is not as evil as that bitch and yet, I don't think she is the *true* evil in this world Ri, I think...I think she is the invisible shield holding it back."

I gave her another keen glance, not expecting Xi to see past her loathing and fear. She was usually a stubborn fae, like the earth, and I loved her for it but perhaps Remnant Dark was the catalyst she needed to pull something out of her I never could.

Peace.

"Shit," she huffed when the flames appeared, several buildings on fire, ash falling like black snow around us. I sensed that there were no other fae here, all had fled.

All except for *one*.

In front of us, a lone shadow fae stood against a tremendous wall of flames that spanned several streets of our little town, incinerating the buildings in its wake with violent, swirling fire. This wasn't just an attack to keep the elemental fae of the plains in line. It was a fucking cleansing.

"They have firestone," Xi breathed as we slowed our pace, walking towards the general who was staring at the wall of flames with trepidation on her smooth porcelain face. The heat from the fire alone was almost intolerable from here. How the general, whose shadows despised any light, was standing mere feet from it was simply astonishing.

My hand brushed against Xi's as we approached, my breathing slightly labored and coming out in a rush, "You must leave, if you go now, they will never know you were here."

She shook her head, "I can sense them beyond the wall, their power combined with the firestone...it's too dangerous. It's unmatched. Besides, it's too late to turn back now."

Dropping my hand away from her I fisted it at my side, the air swirling agitatedly around my arms. "I won't let anything happen to you," I whispered only for her ears.

Sensing us, Remnant Dark looked over her shoulder, her tied back hair blowing wildly in the wind. "Welcome to the fun! Let us get this over with shall we?" Green eyes sparkled while the wall of flames intensified behind her, stretching far into the sky, staining it with smoke and ash. Turning back around, she shifted her stance, widening her legs and raising her arms. "Time to play, my loves," she cooed.

I watched with a mixture of awe and absolute raw fear when the darkness gathered around her, as if it rose from the very bowels of the underworlds of Sheol. Thick, black, rushing shadows whorling higher and higher, not at all hesitant or fearful of the flames licking at their tendrils.

"Be prepared. The shadows will smother these flames but that does not mean what is on the other side isn't equally as dangerous." She glanced back at Xi, "Especially for you."

Xi stiffened beside me and I used my power to caress her bare skin just above the gauntlets she wore. Rock was such an unforgiving element, her manipulation of the stubborn earth often left its mark on her skin, gauntlets deterred this to a degree.

"I'm ready," she said, her voice hard.

The shadow fae assessed her with one last lingering look before nodding, "Yes I think you are." Turning back to the massive wall of shadow that spread up before her like night descending on the town, she smirked. "They always think fire is my weakness. A foolish notion, the darkness is infinite, it has no weaknesses."

"Sweet goddess," Xi breathed as the shadows rose even higher than the flames, blocking out its light and heat, pausing just moments to take a sharp inhale before crashing down in undulating waves. Its power smothering the flames, and extinguishing the fire that had set the buildings ablaze.

"Fucking Sheol," I breathed, the shadows hissing as they fell, spilling outwards like a goddess damn flood, pooling around the full score of barricading elementals that lined the width of the street. I smirked at their best efforts to appear unafraid especially when the darkness lapped at their feet.

Only three were not. In fact, they did not even appear the least bit affected. Two I recognized from the tales that Xi had told me. One male, one female, both with pure white hair, stared back. Their presence sinister and cold—heartless.

The third did not stand, instead he sat perched on a beautiful painted mare, colors of auburn, white, and grey, making up the horse's coat. I narrowed my eyes, nothing about this creature was native to Faerie. It did not even come close to resembling the leathered equine beings with sharp black horns we called nightmares or the grotesque skinless colts of the nuckelavee. Not even the unicorns with their glossy coats and colorful manes came close to this magnificent looking creature, which could only mean one thing.

This horse was a shifter.

A thick, gold collar caught my attention, and I felt my stomach knot with horrific dread, recognizing the tainted power swirling within the adornment and even worse, the fae sitting upon the shifter's beast. Hazel eyes met mine and it was like looking in a mirror. Dark green hair slicked back from a hard-cut face where lips curled in a satisfied smirk.

"I must say," he drolled in his most charming tone while he sat atop the beast like a goddess damn prat. "I hadn't expected a family reunion."

Bile rose and hatred burned, my air swirled violently around me and I was unable to stop myself from stepping alongside the General. If this was what Remnant Dark was fighting against, then I was with her. This bastard belonged in the deepest grave possible—*alive.* Only to give him some semblance of hope that he could survive before I sucked every bit of air from his lungs while he clawed through the earth like the pathetic worm he was.

"Uncle," I hissed.

Dismounting, he laughed at my rage. Flourishing a whip looped at his side, he snapped it against the mare's neck where it latched onto the golden collar, making the beast prance before a bright flash blinded us all. Dressed in soft scarves, the shifter appeared with most of her golden skin on display, long strawberry blonde hair fell down her body to supply some modesty while big, light brown eyes beseeched me to help her.

I could not control the rapid increase of my breath, nor the way my entire body froze, gripped by memories I thought I had overcome. Her eyes, that hair...it was the exact same as my mother's.

Wincing, her sharp cry unfroze my blood and disgust burned in the back of my throat at the cruel way my uncle tugged her by the collar, slamming her into his side possessively. Pawing at her, he smashed her breast into his chest and groped her ass in front of us, his eyes gleaming ruthlessly only at me, knowing I had made the connection between the shifter and my own mother.

"Just like old times, right nephew?" Eyes dancing with mirth, his hand slid up her curvy form to stroke over her hair like a fucking pet, provoking me. But I was no faeling who attacked out of emotion, not anymore. Fisting my hands, I breathed deep, holding my ground as he continued his grating monologue. "I'd give you some loving uncle advice, since we share the same power, and tell you that your decision here today will either keep your head on your shoulders or send it sprawling on the ground so that you may join your parents. But then again, I do love the idea of your head on a pike in front of the city walls."

Xi's soft inhale was the only indication of her shock and I could not bring myself to look at her. My darkest secret now exposed...would she ever understand what I had done after keeping it from her for so long?

The air already stirring violently around me whispered its lethal torrent. I wanted to pull it from his lungs and watch him gasp—suffocating on the very element that would betray him. Except his power was equal to that of my own. It had always been that way...unless our secondary power was used. A tainted monstrous trait, common in our family line. A power that could possess a living being, harnessing their energy to be used by their master, and enhance their skills. One he was currently using on the shifter female he was assaulting right in front of us, unashamed of his vulgar acts.

I hadn't realized I moved until shadows anchored my feet to the ground. I did not need to look down to know they were there, not restraining, but calmly embracing. Their master's hand firmly gripped my shoulder, a touch that was strong and supportive. A slight squeeze that said I'm here for you.

"A fight for another day, Dragoon," Remnant Dark's voice was barely audible but I could hear her all the same. Then she tsked loudly for all to hear, "Now now, Commander Rory Dragoon. There will be no heads on pikes this day unless it's you who is volunteering yours." She smiled sweetly, signaling to the shadows that licked up his body, and my lips twitched.

For the briefest of moments...I saw fear in my uncle's eyes. Something I thought I'd never see.

If I hadn't already decided to join Remnant Ezra Solaire Dark on this quest, then I sure as fucking goddess would have now, just for that moment alone.

I looked back at the shadow fae encased in a halo of darkness, like a deadly savior that dealt justice outside the normal rules of the fae. She had stepped off the game board, lurking in the shadows, waiting for the perfect moment to strike, and I was here for it.

CHAPTER 7

Remnant

P AWNS...WE WERE ALL PAWNS but if one stepped off the board, then they became an unknown, an oddity—dangerous. That was where I liked to play and Riley Dragoon just stepped off the board to play with me.

I felt the shift just moments ago, his acceptance of who and what I was given by the subtle nod he gave me, his eyes changing from fury to understanding.

"You have no power here, General. Only the queen passes out verdicts of death," Rory Dragoon snarled, attempting to hide the flicker of fear in his eyes at the crawling of my shadows.

Giving the commander my fullest attention, my eyes bored into his putrid soul. His aura an oily sludge, smearing over his essence that reeked of nefarious acts and villainous corruption.

Fae like him made the bile rise from my stomach. No honor, no morality, no empathy. As the queen's newly favored fae at court, he had been given the title of Commander of the City of Light.

Nothing but a lackey for her own amusement and boredom, but the twisted air elemental had a thirst for power and took sadistic pleasure in torture even more so than the queen herself.

I had voiced my concerns regarding him many times but Deirdre would not hear of it. No doubt sending him here as an insurance policy and a reminder of where my loyalties lie.

But fae like Rory Dragoon were one of many, Deirdre knew he could be easily replaced...and well...fae died in the plains all the time, *especially* with beasts of origin possibly roaming these lands. I just needed to make sure not a single one of his company survived.

Which would be difficult considering the two fae flanking him were no better, earth elementals with the very stone they wielded for a heart. Soulmates, Fuchai Chin and Xizi Chin, measured close second to Rory in their cruel ways. It was no surprise they were sent along with him.

Granted none of the other fae were innocent either. Faerie far from it. Rory coveted finding his warriors from the bowels of the City of Light where the most corrupt stole, cheated, murdered, and abused the fae around them. It was a goddess damn boon they were all gathered here today, it made my duties to extinguish them an easier task. Coming here was a mistake, one they would never come home from.

I snorted inwardly. Seeing Deirdre's game. Either they found what she wanted or died by my hand, making her look like the valiant queen, eliminating the corruption within her court. Both endings resulted with a triumph for her, such was the boredom of a queen.

"Who said anything about judgment?" With a flick of my wrist, shadows sprouted upwards from their dark flood surrounding us all. "One, two, three, four, now you are no more," I said calmly, my hand rising with each word, sharp spikes of darkness stretching into the cobalt sky, swallowing the fae I had chosen. An executioner of darkness, like the death god himself. "*Lex Talionis*, the law of retribution," I drawled, "for the four fae you murdered here today in their own homes," I added, bringing my hands back to my chest and sucking the darkness inward, I united them into a small swirl of shadow that lovingly draped over my shoulders.

The commander's soldiers converged on themselves, no longer able to save face with death standing before them. They were huddled together like the pathetic fae they were, ready to sacrifice one another to save their own skins.

Riley snickered and I felt the flicker of admiration from his companion who had been silent beside me—understandably so.

Rory Dragoon gurgled, his face turning a satisfying shade of purple and red before outrage bellowed deep from his broad shouldered chest. His fury taken out on the poor shifter he man-handled, throwing her down at his feet, his dark green hair practically vibrating with each word, "You fucking bitch! Those were my warriors, you have no right!"

Forcing myself not to look down at the fae he abused with her big light brown eyes imploring us to help her, I stepped forward, the shadows fanning out from me, my voice calm. "I have every right, *Commander*. This is the fae law of the plains, honored by the queen herself and if you had even an ounce of intelligence you'd know that. Choose your next words to *your* general very, very carefully."

The tall and elegant air elemental standing nearby, Xizi Chin, laughed softly, "Well played Dark."

She smoothed back the fly aways from the tightly knotted bun on the top of her head. A style that accented the beautiful but deadly angles of her face where the dark brown eyes narrowed, "Daughter."

"Xizi." Xi Chin replied calmly, stepping closer beside me in solidarity.

This was...good. I needed Xi Chin on my side. I needed them both. More than I cared to admit. I had been at this for far too long on my own and I could feel the brewing of destiny churning. Something was coming and my task could no longer be done alone.

Five years. *Five years*, I watched them. Xi's aura had drawn me in first but then it was *their* companionship, their loyalty to their people, and their resilience even when everything seemed broken that awed me the most—the markings of true leaders.

"You will address your mother as is her due, Xi Chin." Fuchai Chin, raised his head towards his daughter, his own brown eyes glaring coldly, splitting the earth between us.

The ground rumbled under my own feet, responding in kind to her father's threat, sealing the threatening cracks he had made, Xi glared, "In that case, greetings to you birth bitch, queen of cunts."

My lips twitched and Fuchai's olive skin burned into dark shades I had never seen, his rebuttal sputtering upon thin lips. Opposite, his wife Xizi stood coldly unaffected, the more clever one in the relationship, it was clear she expected this type of greeting from her daughter. A fact that made her dangerous. The commander alone was a nuisance, the commander with Fuchai and Xizi on his side was more than problematic...it was a Faerie fucking disaster.

"I see your vocabulary has not improved, Xi Lanora Chin." With a wave of her hand the earth beneath us calmed, turning towards her sputtering husband, she gave him a soft smile, no love in her eyes. "Do not fret, pet, our daughter has simply forgotten her place." Her gaze sharpened, "She will soon repent for this day."

"I'm not sorry to disappoint you Xizi, but that's just not going to happen." I replied just as smoothly, twirling the shadows between my fingers, "Xi and Riley have been contracted to serve me and my needs until I decide otherwise. Here's hoping you fall into a pit of poisonous dragon plants before then." Shifting my attention back towards the still red faced Rory, I winked at him. "I assume you have been sent for the relic as well. Of course having some competition may require you to use your brain more often...perhaps it will be a good thing for you although you will *still lose.*"

"This isn't over Dark," Rory Dragoon scowled. Snapping his fingers, the shifter cried out before being forced to transform back into her beautiful chestnut mare form.

I smirked, "Oh I am betting on that Commander."

Mounting the horse, he jerked the bit in her mouth hard, the golden collar around the shifter fae's neck glowing again from his control. "You'll regret crossing paths with me, General." He shot over his shoulder, then taking one last look at the air elemental next to me he added, "Next time I see you it'll be on the end of my sword nephew."

Riley Dragoon snorted, "Better make sure it's the sharp pointed end, uncle. I know that confuses you sometimes."

I snickered loudly, my laughter infuriating the commander more, his face as red as his blood I would one day spill. Barking out orders in his fury, the fae scrambled around him, disorganized and still terrified at what I would do next. One dared to look directly into my eyes and I smiled sweetly back, blowing her a kiss, mouthing "You're next", and then laughing at her fearful retreat. She knew I was not playing.

Xizi and Fuchai did not scurry, their retreat made to look more like a choice rather than a necessity, giving us all one last parting look, the air between us stilling with a haunting chill from their combined gazes. Marking us for death.

I snorted loudly, rolling my eyes—it was a futile threat, death was mine to wield and I did it well.

CHAPTER 8

"F UCK. JUST GODDESS DAMN bitch of a Faerie fuck!" I hissed, pacing back and forth amongst the burned mosses of the town that had once been so mystically beautiful. Pausing, I took a deep breath, watching the Goddess River, surrounding the town of Croi, sparkle in the warm rays of the sun as if we hadn't just faced evil in its purest form.

I tugged at the hair in front of my face, trying to control my annoyance and the pounding of my heart. My chest aching from its seizing when I had faced *them*.

Xizi and Fuchai Chin.

I swore I would never give them the pleasure of hurting me again, and here I was pacing like a fearful child, panicking just like before. I hated that they could still do it to me—freeze me in a terror from a time that did not exist anymore. Just their putrid presence and scarce cold words were enough to send me spiraling.

Riley pulled me into him from behind and I sighed, sinking into his warm embrace. His chin rested on the top of my head and his arms squeezed me tightly. I could feel his own frown at the blasted river, likely thinking the same thing I had. It was mocking us. "They are gone now, Xi, and we are under the protection of the General, isn't that right shadow fae?"

Turning in his arms, I studied his gorgeous profile. Wavy green hair fell into his eyes, a strong jaw set determinedly with full pouty lips. Lips I could still feel on my skin from the night before, wishing with every fiber of my being that we were back at the inn, staring up at fake stars, ignoring the world outside.

Remnant shot me a look over Riley's shoulder. "Will it soothe you to know that their deaths are already marked?"

My thudding heart stilled, and Riley's hand squeezed my upper arm, my deep seated hatred hissing through my teeth, "Their deaths are *mine* to deliver, shadow fae."

Dark hair blew across her face, the sun catching the blue sheen amongst the black strands. She smirked, "Excellent, then all will go according to plan." Swiping her hair back, she glanced at the sun, "We should really get moving. Even though Rory is as brilliant as a dust high pixie, with Xizi and Fuchai, he has an edge."

"What kind of edge?" I snapped, brushing off Riley's hand and sending him a sharp look. It was rare for him to show so much affection towards me in public and rare for me to accept it so wholly, something I hadn't realized I was doing until now.

He sighed, giving me a full on pout, hurt flashing in those hazel eyes, and a part of me wanted to fix it. But Riley Dragoon never once claimed me as his and I wasn't about to fall at his feet just because I had the greatest orgy of my life last night. Never mind that it was a one person orgy because with Riley Dragoon that was all you needed.

Shivering with rekindled desire just thinking about what he was capable of, Riley stood taller, his pout gone, knowing exactly where my mind had gone.

I rolled my eyes, tugging my hair again.

"The seal is made of a very specific stone." Remnant answered me at last, seemingly lost in her own thoughts just as Riley and I were lost in each other.

"It's firestone, isn't it?" I shook my head, berating myself for dismissing that thought last night. "There are only three earth elementals that can detect firestone and wield it."

"Yes," she answered simply, arching her back, and stretching her face up to the sun, soaking in its rays. It was such a contrast to see a creature of darkness bask in the glow of the sun but even more so to see it respond. Every bit of the environment around us seemed to worship her. The sparkling river shifted to flow in her direction, the blades of grass bent with her body, the air swirled playfully with the shadows around her. I could even detect the earth reach upwards, the stubborn energy holding her solidly in its steady presence.

The entire world bowed to her darkness as if she were the goddess Faerie herself.

I narrowed my one uncovered eye at her, "Then you know I am one of those three."

Completing her stretching, she grinned at me, "Of course."

Riley whistled in awe and I shot him a look of annoyance.

"So you just want to use me?" I stated simply, feeling bereft. For the briefest of moments, watching our world honor her, I almost allowed myself to forget that she was first and foremost a clever and deadly general to the throne. It was foolish to think I could have ever leaned into her quiet safety of darkness.

Intense eyes firmly held mine and her feet whispered lightly on the green path as she approached me. I stood my ground, my face raised high. "Use you? No, Xi Chin. I need you. You and Riley. This is more than just the retrieval of the seal. This is about the long game...the survival of all our people."

Shocked by her confession, I licked at my bottom lip, "*Our* people?"

Her hand reached out to grasp my shoulder, and despite her short stature, I felt small under her firm grip, "Yes Xi, our people." She looked between us, her tone suddenly light and cheerful. "Alright, so what is the quickest and least conspicuous way to Lacail?"

I glanced at Riley, and his brow raised. She couldn't know? Could she? "I might know a route we can take."

"Good," she said, falling away, then frowned at the glittering river as if something dangerous lurked beneath the surface, "I'd rather avoid my quickest route."

Tracking her pensive gaze towards the water, I saw nothing that seemed out of place despite the fact that the flow of it fucking changed direction wherever she walked. The water's reflected light dancing across her musing profile.

I sighed, hoping we weren't going to regret this, "Why Lacail? My bastard parents and that Commander with his cronies went north, Lacail is south."

Shaking her head, Remnant Dark hummed. "You don't win the game by following others, Xi Chin. You win by making your own rules."

Riley snorted, "I believe that is called cheating."

The shadow fae war general laughed and walked away, waving for us both to follow, "A fae's favorite past time...or do you call it deceiving. In any case you'd be foolish to trust that any fae would not cheat, and I believe that is *exactly* what we need to do," she replied impishly, delight sparkling in her eyes when she glanced back over her shoulder.

"I have a bad feeling about this...that tone, did you hear it this time Ri?" I hissed, when more space grew between us and the general, my head leaning into Riley while we followed the shadow fae down the mossy lane, untouched by the brutal fire that destroyed a quarter of the town. It would be a ghost town for a few more days, before any fae felt safe enough to return here. As such, Riley and I rarely ever stayed in one place. Faerie was vast, and so were its adventures and its woes. Since the wars, we had done everything in our power to experience one and assist with the other.

Shadows popping in our faces brought us both to a stuttering halt. Wide eyed, I held my breath, watching them swirl and shimmer, circling around our legs like a cat purring for a scratch. Except they were no feline housepet, these were deadly entities, made even more terrifying by their sentient nature.

Remnant looked back over her shoulder, her mouth stretched into a knowing grin. "They like you. Give them a pet, they love it," she called out to us.

Rising in front of me, a single dark cloud morphed to hover at eye level—waiting. Wide eyed, I watched Riley's hand reach out to them. "Hey ummm, shadows," he stammered, eyeing the way they glittered...happily?

Inhaling deeply I followed, knowing that we were stuck with them for the task ahead and I would be better off if I just accepted their terrifying nature in a cordial way. "Hi," I said simply, letting my fingers gently touch their inky tendrils, shuddering at the coolness but in awe of the soothing quiet of their presence. Just like their master.

They swirled and I gasped, snapping my hand back, except they did not stop. Swarming, they flitted around me almost playfully, rustling my hair, and caressing my body with their dark soft touch.

"They said hi already, my loves, and you know you are scaring the elementals more. Enough playing, we still have places to be," Remnant cooed out to them, already halfway down the street from us.

The shadows disappeared and reappeared at her side in an instant, drawing a small laugh from their owner. Carefree and light, this was a version of the general of Faerie I would have never expected to ever see. Granted, her eyes did shine with love for instruments of death, but we were fae, who were we to judge, death was the end result of most of our power.

Bemused, I stared after them. "Goddess, is it too early to say that I kind of like those little shadow fiends?" I whispered.

Riley snorted, tilting his chin for us to walk and I followed him. "If only they swallowed up my uncle and your parents instead." His dark green brows drew in thoughtfully.

Watching the sauntering shadow fae with dreaded suspicion, I whispered from the corner of my mouth, "I have a feeling she planned it that way. She wants them alive for some reason."

From my periphery, Riley nodded, "Yes...except that shifter fae will suffer for it."

I glanced at him sharply. "What was that about Ri? How could he control her that way and why did we not stop it? Why did he say you both have the same power?"

The muscles of his face clenched, his jaw grinding hard. "Because it can't be stopped, if their control is broken then the poor girl will die. The general knew this." He paused, struggling to find words before blowing out a long sigh, "Xi...what you saw, it is a secondary power that everyone wields in my family line, including me."

Grabbing onto his shoulder, I spun him to face me, halting us in the middle of the street with the mocking sun highlighting the absolute horror on my face. "What? I thought he was just taunting you. What do you mean you wield the same power Ri? Please tell me you have never bound someone like that?"

He grimaced and I pushed him away from me in disgust, his large lithe body stumbling backwards, eyes flashing me a look of hurt. He *knew* what this would do to me. I had lived too long under the cruel servitude of my own family. I shook my head vehemently. "No. Not you. You're not like them...tell me you're not like them!" I shrieked.

CHAPTER 9

FLINCHING, THE SHRILL PITCH of her tone was worse than being pierced by an arrow. I had hoped, prayed even, that if I buried my terrible secret long enough it wouldn't be real and Xi would never have to know what I had done.

I stumbled on my words like a fool, watching a kaleidoscope of pain, shock, and rage morph across half of her revealed face. How could I possibly make her see...it was never a choice to have this terrible power. For the fae, the most powerful of them evolved, their traits transcending into something uniquely their own. It did not belong to a faction or a court or a people or even a goddess who created us. It was just ours. Unfortunately, mine was naught but a fucking curse, one I had to use to save her and damn us.

"Of course he isn't like them, Xi Chin." Remnant Dark in-terjected, mystically between us with raised brows, her hand set firmly on her hips, and the shadows swirling around her agitatedly, "Don't let your own fear tarnish what you two have." Sighing she shook her head, "I am sure Riley has an explanation," she gave me a pointed look, "but it is one we must save for now, we *really* need to go." Her eyes falling off us towards the river with lips pressed in a thin line.

Following her sight, I narrowed my eyes on the whirlpool churning in the river nearby, "Is that—?"

"The water fae are coming," Remnant nodded, grabbing our arms and hurrying us along swiftly, away from the river-bend.

Xi scowled, snapping at the shadow fae, "And *what* exactly are we walking into with such haste and since when is any fae fearful of the water fae?"

Unfazed, Remnant pursed her lips while a subtle breeze swirled her hair, pausing its cooling current to honor her—something I had never seen air do before unless manipulated by an elemental. Sweet goddess, Faerie gravitated towards this fae like she was its very heartbeat. "I believe the next beast of origin will be unleashed, that is what we are walking into—and only a fool would not be wary of the water fae, Xi Chin. Do I look like a fool to you?" she snapped.

"It's still to be determined," Xi snarled back and a smile twitched at the shadow fae's lips from her sharp quip.

Seeing the truth shifting in the general's emerald eyes, my brows raised, "You believe the twin seal has weakened already?"

"Yes, I do," she muttered, head tilting towards a soft chirp on a low rooftop where a lone chickadee hopped along the edge, agitated and restless.

Xi refused to meet my wayward glance but I knew what she was thinking, that this shadow fae was crazy. Normally, I would have agreed but there was just something about *that bird*...something that felt like we should listen.

Shaking my head to release the strange feeling, I sighed, "Lacail it is then."

"I'll gather my things," Xi barked, stomping towards the direction of the tavern, and I knew it wasn't just Remnant she wanted to escape from. Her fury towards me was palpable on the fucking air.

"No need and no time," Remnant said cheerily, but I did not miss the way she glanced at the water one more time. "I took the liberty of having the shadows gather your things."

My arms crossed in front of my chest and I smirked at the innocent expression on her face. "When exactly did you have time for that?"

The General shrugged. "This morning when you joined me for breakfast."

My stomach rumbled at the thought of the food we had left behind on the table.

Xi huffed, "And where exactly is our stuff then."

Goddess damn, she was in a mood. I wasn't even fucking sure how I was going to fix it but I sure as Sheol wasn't going to lose her, not over something I had no control over.

Remnant indicated the shadows trailing after her. "Ask and you shall receive."

Cracking my neck to the side, I grinned, needing to feel the solace of my parent's blades since the past was so eager to haunt me. "In that case, I'd like my scimitars..." I paused, peering at the endless void of darkness, hating that I wondered what was really within them. Was it truly a non-existence or was there something else, something *alive*? "Please."

Xi snorted, but her laughter was comically cut short when blades were expelled from the darkness like thrown javelins. Reacting quickly, I spun my element, slowing their descent, and catching them lightly in my hand, relishing the sound of steel cutting through the air. A delicate hiss that was almost as sweet as the one I drew out of Xi last night.

Grinning, I winked at the shadows. "Thanks...uh...what do you call them exactly?"

Remnant shrugged. "My loves, darkness..." she smiled widely at me, her brilliant green eyes glittering, "death."

"Uh...right," I drawled, caught by the intensity of her dark humorous gaze, and sheathing the swords at my back.

"Well if we are in such a rush to run from water fae, then why don't we get moving," Xi grumbled, not finding any amusement in our current predicament while I was fucking coming alive. I could feel it simmering, the excitement and anticipation—new challenges, new risks, new friendships, new truths. I glanced over at my glowering friend-lover, lover-friend, or whatever we were, perhaps we could finally be free to be both now... if I just had the time to explain.

Remnant nodded, "Right, do your thing then...I am curious to know how you disappeared so easily from the City of Light."

Xi grinned widely, her singular grey eye sparkling with dark intent.

"Shit. Don't do it Xi." I took one step too late. Goddess damn it, this wasn't just a mood, it was a whole new vibe—one we were about to pay for. I groaned as my foot sunk straight into the earth. I hated it when she did this.

Falling through the fastest quicksand I had ever had the displeasure of being a victim to, I held my breath instinctively while the earth swallowed me whole within seconds.

Suffocation. A horrible ironic way for an air elemental to find himself and yet here I was, the pressure of the earth condensing my body, the ground so thick that there was only the air left in my lungs for my power to manipulate. I cursed heavily inside my mind as we sunk deeper still, wondering how the shadow fae general was faring and what kind of repercussions I would face in defense of my partner for her latest stunt.

Feeling suddenly weightless, I dropped from the earth, landing in a quiet crouch, deep into a very large cavernous tunnel. Slowly standing at the vicious cursing of Remnant Dark.

The shadow fae had already passed through the earth moments before me and was currently spitting out dirt with disgust.

"Goddess damn it, Xi Chin," she cursed, summoning what looked like a canteen from her shadows. My assumption was proven correct when the sound of water sloshing in her mouth became the only sound within the tunnel.

Holding back my laughter, I listened to the general of Faerie rinsing and spitting out water in rapid succession. Any proper decorum she may have had was truly lost, continued curses along with the forceful expulsion of dirt from her body enough to make any fae recoil. "I know there was a better way of doing that." Sticking out her tongue and smacking her lips. "I'm going to be tasting dirt for days."

Xi's dark laughter behind us revealed that she had been there all along, quietly watching with retribution in the darkness and damn it if I didn't find her quiet stalking sexy.

Running my hand through my hair, I shook out the lingering dirt, hearing it rain down on the smoothly carved tunnel floor. "Welcome to my eternal version of Sheol, General." I muttered, shaking out more dirt from my pant leg and wincing at the fact that there was sand grating against my ball sack right the fuck now.

"Shall we get moving? You did say we were in a hurry, general?" Xi said sweetly, brushing by me aggressively, throwing her shoulder into my body as she went.

Evidently, burying me alive wasn't enough for her to forgive me.

Remnant Dark narrowed her eyes at the fae walking by her. "Why do I have a feeling *that* tone is never a good one?"

I chuckled darkly, flicking off a large chunk of dirt still caked on the shadow fae's shoulder. "Because it's fucking not."

She pursed her lips, throwing her canteen upwards for the shadows to engulf and I blinked at the messed up way that simple act stirred an admiring fear inside of me. "I blame you for this, Riley Dragoon."

Sidestepping, I waved towards the darkened tunnel Xi had already disappeared into, frowning after her but keeping my tone lighthearted, "You'll fit right in here then, General. After you."

Grumbling under her breath about fucking elementals and still spitting out grit, Remnant trailed after Xi. I cursed inwardly with her, my hands curling the air into fists at my sides.

Fuck me to Sheol and back, I now had drawn the ire of two of the most powerful fae of Faerie. If I came out of these tunnels unscathed it would be a goddess damn miracle.

Chapter 10

Remnant

Humming, I trailed my fingers along the darkened tunnel, admiring the carved earth and the amount of power it must have taken to create such a place. Skimming between my fingers, the shadows danced along the walls, following our quiet party with their own darkened silence.

And silent we remained, for the next *twelve* hours, not for the lack of trying by Riley Dragoon. His attempts to mend the hurt his secret had caused was met by a cold shoulder and more than a few rocks being thrown his way.

As for me, I had more self preservation than the air elemental, not relishing the idea of being target practice, my inner thoughts stayed my own. Although, any fool could see that despite the fury still rolling off Xi Chin, these two were kismet. Their breaths, their strides, their heartbeats were one and I highly doubted one misunderstood secret would break what fate had already preordained.

I glanced at the silhouette of Xi Chin leading the way, perhaps it was time to try another tactic, "Is this entire tunnel quartz?" The hushed silence broke as I relished the luxurious feel of the cool smooth slide of my fingertips on the tunnel wall.

A flicker of pause before Xi's voice answered with surprise, "You know your stone by touch alone?"

"I may have done some training in the Argenti Caves..." I said while marveling at the tunnels. I left out the fact that *some training* had actually been more like a half of a century. Trapped in the cave mines, Gaib Castella left no room for error, the knowledge of stone, elements, metals, and minerals were to be mastered in order to create even a single blade. Riley whistled behind me and Xi's steps faltered, "Argenti Caves? That means you know Gaib Castella?"

I snorted and rolled my eyes, dropping my hand from the wall. "Does anyone really know Gaib Castella? In the fifty years it took me to perfect one blade to his standards, I learned no more about him than when I had first arrived."

This time the light step of Riley's stride wavered slightly, the rhythm suddenly off from his partner's. "You have your own steel from the Argenti caves?" he whispered reverently.

I flashed him a grin in the dark. "Daggers, throwing daggers."

Riley chuckled with dark amusement. "I knew there was something special about that blade you allowed Caval to throw at you..."

"How observant of you Riley Dragoon, and yes, you are correct, that was one of them."

"One," Xi inhaled, finally joining in, "you have more?"

I snickered, "Breathe my friends, yes I have more, eight to be exact. You always need at least one set. After all, some targets are just so much more satisfying with multiple blades stuck in them." I could think of more than a few fae that deserved this fate. Starting with both their relatives.

A low rumble followed shortly by the slightest sound of stone splitting broke my dark vengeful thoughts. I spun to reach out to the wall, feeling the slight splinter on the hardened surface. "It's breaking," I gasped.

"Fuck," Xi spat. Brushing by me, she knocked my hand away, spreading both her own against the wall. "Something...is wrong," she shook her head. "It's not an earth elemental though. I can't detect any other power but ours here."

Stepping around her, I narrowed my eyes into the deep abyss of the tunnel. "How close are we to Lacail?"

"About a two day's walk in these tunnels," Xi whispered, as the rumbling grew, reminding me too goddess damn much of a roaring stampede. More stone splintered around us.

"Can you take us to the surface?" I questioned, summoning the shadows. The tunnel itself was expansive, more than quadruple my height and wide enough for five fae to walk shoulder to shoulder. Wide enough for even monsters to traverse.

Distant roaring joined the rumbling with speckled quartz sprinkling down upon our heads. I hated it when I was right sometimes.

"What in the Faerie fuck is that?" Riley hissed, stepping behind me, shaking the dust from his hair.

"Goddess if I know," Xi snapped, "We have used these tunnels many times before and never have had any trouble and never heard a sound quite like that. And no, General, we cannot just go to the surface. We are directly under Lac Asrai."

I raised my brows, staring into the darkness, sending my shadows searching forward. "You created a tunnel under the largest lake in Faerie."

A long pause. "Yes?"

"Knowing that it is also the most enchanted, unstable lake in Faerie."

Silence, then a small whisper, "Yes."

I grinned into the darkness, more than wonderstruck. "Well that's just goddess impressive isn't it? How many of these tunnels exist exactly?" My love for this world and the creatures within it revived by its ability to still surprise me. There was nothing like Faerie and there never would be again. If we didn't find a way to preserve it then it would be only a matter of time before we would all become lost. A beautiful, bright star, once admired by all, dimming and fading into darkness, never to be remembered.

I could not accept that this was our only fate, because then what was it all for? The battle, the sacrifice, the hope, the love. No. These were all things that were still worth fighting for—Xi and Riley exemplified every bit of this and that was enough to ensure I carried on.

"We said we would help you," Riley Dragoon cut in, no doubt trying to win over his lover's good favor again, "We did not say we would give you all our secrets."

I snickered but it was cut short as another roaring rumbled, closer this time and not stopping. A grotesque stench assaulted us shortly after, sending me stumbling backward from its repugnant scent. A scent I had the misfortune of experiencing only one other time...when my brother unleashed the trolls from their cursed stone in the queen's throne room.

"Damn me to Sheol and back, what in the goddess is that smell?" Dragoon coughed behind me.

My lips pressed into a thin line, my nose wrinkling with disgust. "Trolls, Dragoon. Specifically troll *ass*." The sound of choked laughter echoed from behind me while I stretched my arms over my head, drawing my blade from the shadows. "Stay here. I'll take care of this before they end up bringing down the tunnel upon us."

"By the sound and the smell of it, there is more than one troll, General Dark. It's a fucking stampede of them," the air elemental exclaimed.

Glancing over my shoulder, I winked at him through the darkness. Whether he saw it or not did not matter, the tone of my voice said it all. "That's the fun of it, Dragoon. Just stay here and I'll be back in a few." Turning towards Xi, I added, "Keep the tunnel from collapsing. This may be quartz but troll clubs are enchanted to break through any stone and earth...I'd rather not have the whole of Lac Asari collapsing down on me." Striding forward with my sword raised, I added under my breath, "Drowning is never that much fun."

Walking into the darkness, the smell becoming more and more concentrated, I heard Xi's whisper. "Did she just insinuate she drowned before?"

I grinned, certain that by dinner time they would have their shit worked out. They were too interwoven, too connected to stay at odds with each other.

"Maybe it was a metaphor," Riley whispered back, his words following me through the tunnel where more roars and distant grunts could be heard. Weaving shadows around my head, before my eyes burned from the smell, I heard Xi's last words.

"I'm also starting to hate it when she uses that tone...like the world is ending but no worries, we will all die a glorious death."

My eyes gleamed in the darkness. If the world did indeed end one day, our deaths would be more than glorious—they would be eternal.

Chapter 11

RILEY SHIFTED UNCOMFORTABLY WHILE we watched Remnant fade into the darkness, and I found myself wishing she would come back, if only to save me from the awkward silence between us.

I was hurt and confused, afraid of the answers to the questions burning in my mind. Who had he used his power on? Why? When? What happened to them? Did he kill them? And as these thoughts echoed over and over in my head, none of the answers Riley could possibly have seemed adequate enough and that...terrified me.

"Xi—" he attempted but was cut off by a sudden sonic blast bursting from the far reaches of the tunnel. Flying backwards, I grunted when I hit Riley's solid body, his hands firmly gripping my shoulders to place me back on my feet while we both gagged on the sudden concentration of that vile smell the general so lovingly called *troll ass*.

But that wasn't the worst of our worries, no it could never be that simple. Like a quake that broke the surface of the earth, the sound of quartz cracking and the thunderous booms of large slabs of stone caving in all around us was terrifying.

"Shit!" I screamed, my knee slamming into the floor, my hands slapping against the smooth surface while I gritted my teeth, willing the stone to mend. My eyes widened, feeling the utter destruction of the tunnel itself and the pressure of the lac above, trickles of water already seeping into the stoney layers. Pouring more power into it, I cursed again. It was too much, compromised almost beyond saving.

I snarled, *almost*. I wasn't about to let the one thing that had been my salvation and my freedom end so tragically. If I did, then what was it all fucking for? The never ending training, the tortured labor to build character, the faeling dreams of escaping, the hopes to one day be stronger so that I would have my vengeance and take back my life.

"How can I help?" Riley knelt beside me.

Turning to face him, I was close enough to see the anxious lines on his handsome face, knowing that it wasn't for the worry of being buried alive, but out of concern for me. It pissed me off. "If I refuse your help will you collar me and force my hand?" The words escaped venomously from my lips.

Green brows furrowed together, hazel eyes flashing with hurt and anger. "Be angry at me all you want now terrella but not at the sacrifice of your own life. Please. Tell me how I can help, and when this is over, I promise, I will give you the answers you seek, I will walk away if that is what you wish but only when I know you are goddess damn safe."

Eyes watering with bitter tears, I whispered the truth while my heart broke for the tunnel and what was already beginning to feel like the loss of him, "I won't be able to hold it back."

More roars and bellows, thunderous booms, and falling rocks surrounded us, all of which Riley ignored, his gaze never leaving mine. The air stirred and I closed my eyes against the familiar calming feel of it while my hair was brushed back from my face. Snapping my eyes back open, I stared straight into Riley's glowing hazel ones, two perfect andalusite gems, ones that I could horde like a dragon, peering deeply into for the rest of my life. I wasn't sure if I could ever let him walk away but also was not sure if I could ever stay. His entire body leaned towards me as we shared one breath. "I got you terrella and I always will even if you don't want it."

I gasped when violent forces of air exploded all around us and I sighed with partial relief. The combination of Riley's pressurized air and my earth powers forced the stone to shift back in place and the cracks to mend, taking the strain off my body but not my heart.

That was us, an unlikely pair of elements weathering the storms, manipulating our fate with air and earth—smoothing surfaces tarnished and blemished by scars and broken dreams.

Except those dreams were slipping away.

Ear-splitting roars, a thunderous crash, and another shuddering quake through the tunnel tore our gazes from each other and we peered deep into the darkness where large mounded forms appeared.

Riley's eyes narrowed. "Something is coming and coming in fast."

I nodded in agreement, I could feel and hear the forceful skid of a creature heading quickly in our direction. Steel glinted in the darkness as Riley drew his scimitars, its metal sliced through the air.

Our breaths collectively held as the sliding sound came to a forceful squeaking halt right at our kneeled bodies. Riley's blades were poised across a pale throat, emerald green eyes encased in a halo of dark hair sparkled from the general of Faerie.

I blinked slowly with understanding, Remnant Dark had been fucking thrown several feet back through the tunnel and had ended up sliding across the quartz to be delivered at our feet.

"Oh hello, *amicis.*"

Friends. I blinked again, she had just called us *friends* in ancient fae.

"Fucking goddess," Riley cursed, quickly removing his blades.

A feral grin of her white teeth flashed in the darkness. "That didn't quite go according to plan," she snickered, "I can't imagine why? Even the shadows attempted to slightly coerce them."

I quirked a brow down at her. "Slightly?" Goddess help us, this could not be the deadly general they recounted terrifying stories about to keep fae in line—she was...she was...

"One of us," Ri finished my unspoken thought but there was worry underlining his words...because for now there really wasn't an us. Snapping his hand down with a masking chuckle, he held it before Remnant Dark. "Need any assistance, General?"

Grunting, she clasped hands with Riley and we all stood in one fluid movement, facing the roars that were getting closer and closer to where we stood. Sighing, Remnant straightened her leather vest, sweeping her hair back from her face and giving me a quick second look. "Not to make you uncomfortable or anything, but did you know that you are absolutely irrevocably stunning with your hair back?"

Riley choked next to me and I felt my eyes widen more than they had when I first saw her gazing up at us after having been tossed like a sack of potatoes by fucking trolls.

Grasping my hair, I flung it back over my face. "I hardly think that should be the point of our conversation, General. The tunnel is caving in and I can't stop it quickly enough to fight trolls. Riley's air is the only thing holding it back from fully collapsing..." The burn of bitter emotion seared my throat as I spoke that truth aloud for a second time today.

"That's not all," she added, pressing her lips together and shaking her head, "these trolls. They are protected somehow, my shadows can't touch them."

I sputtered despite myself. I had seen her shadows take down possessed spirits from beyond the veil. There was absolutely nothing that could ever defeat them. "What do you mean your shadows can't touch them, what kind of power can do that?"

I could just make out her shrug in the darkness. "No idea but killing them is out of the question."

"I'm sorry," I added dryly, "did I just hear you say you don't plan to kill the horde of trolls trying to annihilate us by bringing this tunnel down on our heads?"

Green eyes sent me a sharp look. "Whatever has shielded them has also hurt them, it is driving them feral." She shrugged again. "Besides you would be mad too if you were a giant troll stuck in a tunnel with no end in sight and smelled like that."

On cue Riley gagged. "Not to break up this lovely tête-à-tête," his nose wrinkled with disgust, "but I am pretty sure we better come up with a plan soon because I can't take another moment of this putrid air."

Tilting his chin to the tunnel, we could see the clear outline of darkened shapes charging towards us, clubs bashing against the walls, their escalating howls and sweet goddess—red eyes? Trolls did not have red eyes. This must have been what the General had meant by *protected*.

I shivered when a deep sense of foreboding shot up my spine. I was never one to ignore these kinds of feelings. It was a warning…of something beyond our understanding, something I didn't want to know.

CHAPTER 12

R EMNANT DARK SIGHED—A SIGH I had heard many times in my life, one that said, *I can't believe I'm about to fucking say this but...*

"Well I didn't want to have to resort to this but—it's time for a swim." She looked around the tunnel reluctantly with an air of sadness.

And *there* it goddess damn was.

Xi practically sputtered, but before anyone could respond, the horde of trolls charged, and I cursed. Shoving the shadow fae back against Xi, I stepped forward focusing the pressurized air towards their massive forms. They were close enough now that I could just make out the glint of their large tusks, wiry-haired bodies, and thick, trunk-like arms carrying spiked clubs scraping across the marbled ground.

Barely feet away, my eyes watered at their rancid smell, knowing that enough concentration of their stench had the ability to knock a fae unconscious for days. Blasting air from my out-stretched hands, the gale forces hit the leading troll directly in the chest, sending him roaring backwards, crashing thunder-ously into the other five. In perfect domino sequence, they all tumbled one by one back down the tunnel—-and thank the fucking goddess they took their ass fetor with them.

Snickering over their infuriated roars, I said dryly over my shoulder, "Well, would you look at that, the trolls are on the roll."

Xi groaned and I considered myself lucky that she was even talking to me, her words from just moments ago haunting me. *Will you collar me and force my hand...*

Unable to contain myself, the stress of the situation too great for me to handle, I added with an even wider grin, "It's a nice day for a troll stroll wouldn't you say?" I shrugged animat-edly, "Just trolling around here. Perhaps when we get tired we can settle down for a nice cuppa tea and a quaint game of troll bowl."

Remnant Dark giggled behind me, "Trolling..." she repeat-ed with an amused murmur.

Xi hissed, "Are you two serious right the fuck now?"

"As serious as a toll from a troll," I added, the sweat pour-ing down my brow from the massive amounts of power I was using. I watched the dark shapes smashing against the walls and wrestling over one another to rise. Their exertion and clumsi-ness generating a series of goddess awful flatulence that had me gagging on my own laughter from the grotesque smell.

"Dragoon!" Xi hissed at me in warning.

"Hey Riley?" Remnant stepped next to me smiling, "What do you call a troll in a bubble?"

I grinned madly at her, "I don't know General, what *do you* call a bubbled troll?"

"Your next job, Dragoon." She slapped my shoulder, her white teeth flashing in the dark, "Time to get to work. I can't touch them but obviously your air can, place a sphere of air around those bastards and let's get the goddess out of here! I'd rather not go down in history as the shadow fae that asphyxiated on troll farts in a collapsed tunnel."

"No, no, no," Xi said, turning towards me, her bright sin-gular eye pleading with me to find another way.

Remnant's tone was sympathetic, "I'm sorry Xi, we played it your way, now it's time to play mine. This tunnel will not last."

Pulling the shadows around her, they began to swirl in a dark cyclone, and she pressed her lips into a thin line looking up at the ceiling. Mesmerized by the darkness, I jumped back when suddenly her sentient ones popped in front of me, from the goddess only knew where, and then circled a thin veil of shadow around us. Shielding us from what their master was about to do next.

Xi sighed sadly next to me

"Here goes nothing," I murmured, gritting my teeth against the sorrow I felt coming from my partner and refocusing on the air I used to brace the tunnel around the trolls, encapsulating them inside. Roaring and fighting, they rolled and tumbled, striving to reach us but unable to break the barrier around them.

The tunnel began to quake, slabs of stone falling in rapid succession, crumbling around both bubbled shields of air and shadow while great sprays of water broke through, filling the tunnel rapidly with the cold enchanted waters of Lac Asrai.

"No!" Xi cursed within our shadow bubble, her body trembling violently, still keeping her hold on the tunnel to prevent its total destruction.

"Let go Xi!" Remnant screamed, throwing shadow around herself before her darkness blasted upwards, swallowing the quartz, the soft earth, the lakebed, and the water itself. A beam of darkness shooting straight into the welcomed sight of cobalt skies, devouring everything in its path.

Sweat poured down Xi's temple, her hair falling over her face once more. Her uncovered eye wide, she shook harder with exertion. She still had yet to let go of her element and was single handedly holding the tunnel intact against the collapsing earth, against an entire damn body of water. The immensity of her power was fearsomely beautiful—but so was the fae wielding it. A tear fell down the side of her face, mingling with the sweat, and I knew if I pulled her hair back, I'd see the mirror image on the other side.

Remnant had no way of knowing...no way of understanding that this, at one time, was Xi's sanctuary. The tunnels she built were an escape. The way she had freed herself from the abuse of her home, the cruelty of her parents. A young faeling...living deep beneath the earth, burying her pain with each layer of stone, healing and becoming stronger all by herself. Alone in this world—my secrets had only made her feel that forsakenness all over again.

Reaching out, I tilted her chin upwards so that she looked into my eyes, wiping the lone tear away. "Let go, my terrella. If you'll have me, one day we will build it again, this time together, and it will be in love, not in pain, not in fear but in pure everlasting love. The strongest thing this world has to offer, better than any stone."

"Ri," she whispered brokenly.

I leaned in, pausing just before my lips touched hers, waiting for permission, waiting to see if she would accept me in all her anger, confusion and distrust. "Let go Xi." I whispered against her quivering mouth.

Her grey eye searched mine, but she knew as much as we all did. Fae did not lie. This was the closest I had ever come to telling her just how much I goddess damn loved her and she could see it on my face, the sweet whisper from my lips, the way my hand held firm on her trembling body.

She nodded, closing her eyes, lashes fluttering against the pained expression on her face before she pressed her lips into mine and the tunnel caved. A sob tore from her soul and I swallowed it down. Crushing her to me, I held her grieving body, and latched onto the bubble of air the trolls were encased in while Remnant blasted us out of the sudden roaring rush of water and earth.

Flying momentarily into the air like the spray from a goddess damn geyser, we crashed onto the reedy shores of the lake, covered with thick roots and large leafy palms.

The shadows broke upon impact, sending us careening in a tumbled mess over each other. Contorting my body, I rolled, holding Xi tight as my exposed back scraped harshly along mud, reeds, and small trees. Bouncing like a fucking ball as I came to a firm stop, Xi still secure atop of me.

Just beyond I dropped the trolls in their bubble of air into the lake. Groaning, I stared up into Xi's face, hovering just inches from mine.

Laughing shakily, I reached up, brushing back her hair to gaze at her stunning beauty that stole even my own fucking air, leaving me defenseless. For this...for her, I would gratefully suffocate. Smiling softly, I whispered huskily with what remaining breath I had, "Hey you."

She inhaled, then her lips crashed into mine again, and this time I groaned for a whole different reason. Hands threading through my hair, her tongue swept into my mouth and I opened for her. She tasted of ambrosia and the fresh chilling wind, and it consumed all of me. Her dominant claim of my body made me desperate for more and I relished every second of it before her sensibilities came back to her and she remembered that I was a monster. A greedy one. For if she chose to keep me, to still love me...I would drown in that feeling for all of time, even if it left me bereft and weak.

Stiffening, as if she felt my words, she ripped her mouth away from mine. Straddling my body with fury, she inhaled deeply, and when the breath left her swollen lips, the harsh whisper was a shot through my heart. "No."

Scrambling to stand, she replicated the physical distance that her refusal of me had created.

Unable to look at her broken expression, I closed my eyes painfully, the last of my confidence in being able to explain my power escaping me just as quickly as she did from my arms.

Chapter 13

Remnant

I stood awkwardly on the lapping shores of Lac Asrai staring at tussling trolls encased in a bubble of air floating along the soft waves. Their roars had been drowned out by the tightly sealed air of Riley's impressive power, but even so, a herd of camphor nearby danced away from the water's edge, enraptured by the comical scene but wary of what it may mean. I shared their wariness having never seen a creature repel shadow like the trolls did in that cave. The fact that the air elemental power worked on them and still held them prisoner was quite admirable, but confused me even more.

When moans and gasps were heard behind me, I grinned, giving the elemental twins space and walking away closer to the waters edge. I was fairly certain I wouldn't be invited to this particular party and there were no hard feelings there. If I was blessed to love someone the way those two loved one another, there would be no goddess damn way I'd share them with someone else.

Pacing the lac's shores, I focused back on the strange red light in the troll's eyes. Pondering again on what kind of power could repel mine.

Seemingly unperturbed by this, the shadows themselves floated lazily beside me, their cloud of darkness shimmering from the reflected light on the tranquil surface of the lac. I bit my lip as I stared up into the sun, somehow always finding its brightness both calling and mocking. As if I was born to bask in some sort of light even if all of me was darkness and shadows.

These past hundred years had been full of trials. First, I was abandoned by my family following the vows I made to serve the throne. Then, Deirdre's cold withdrawal from what was once an intimate love was enough to throw me off balance. I had foolishly thought I could rebuild Faerie and still fall in love with her dangerous silver beauty, but it was becoming more and more apparent that there was very little love left in her heart...even if I did think at one time, mine would have been enough to see us through. But I was never enough, not enough for her, and not even enough for my own family. The sting from their abandonment even sharper the further Deirdre drew away.

When the soft chirp of a chickadee fluttered nearby and my shadows blocked my penetrating stare at the lac, I looked between them both with raised brows. "I know what you both are trying to tell me," I said wistfully. The shadows gently brushed against my face while the bird above chirped again. "We haven't spoken for so long. I don't know if she would even respond."

Time was funny for immortals. Decades felt like only months, centuries like years but even with that said, the last time I had spoken to my mother, Lady Eve Dark, leader of the shadow fae court, felt like a distant memory. A painfully distant one.

When a song broke out, I looked up to glare at the warbling bird. "For goddess sake, you're going to alert every living thing that I am here! Yes, yes, I get it already but there is no guarantee that she will even know what the goddess this shit is—"

"So we are talking to birds now are we?" Xi called, her voice tense and sharp.

The shadows shimmered around me, swirling over my head as my gaze snapped back down to the approaching fae. Xi's face was flushed but it was not the complexion of a fae who was in love. No—it was one of continued hurt and anger and beside her, Riley followed in his own defeat. His shoulders slumped, fists clenched at his sides, the air stirring his hair agitatedly.

Inwardly I groaned. Goddess help me, they *still* had not worked their shit out and it took just one look at the crossed arms of the stubborn earth elemental in front of me to understand why. Damn elementals.

"Birds, shadows," I jerked my chin up to the chickadee that chirped one more time before retreating to the skies. "It doesn't matter, I listen to all of Faerie."

Xi tilted her head, her white hair falling back over her stunning grey eyes and flawless olive skin. Her fitted green shirt and brown leathers were all back in order as well, minus her gauntlets she must have discarded. "But that is a bird, not the goddess, am I missing something?"

Twirling my hands within the smokey tendrils of the shadows, they followed the ink of my tattoos, reminding me of my vows to the darkness that were etched into my skin. Biting at my lip with indecision before I answered. "Faerie is within all...even just a bird. A wise fae will heed her voice no matter how small or distant they may be."

Xi snorted, "And what is this voice telling you then?"

I sniffed, turning back towards the thick tropical trees bordering the lac. "I need to contact my mother...and there is something not right about this jungle. A chickadee hardly ever chooses open skies rather than the cover of the woods."

Together, we all peered into the thick foliage where huge, moss-covered trees with thick vines hanging from their boughs and white butterflies peeking between their dense leaves stretched wide and far. It called to us in a haunting way, one that should have made us turn back in the other direction...but that wasn't an option now. We were here and we had to go through this jungle to get to Lacail.

"So what about the trolls?" Riley drawled, tilting his head to the side, the slight strain to his power crinkling at the corner of his eyes. So he did have limits, this was good to know, a fae that did not, was a fae easily corrupted by power. I had about enough of those.

I sighed heavily, turning back towards the bobbing trolls, "I was hoping that whatever was controlling them would have worn off by now but it seems that isn't the case."

"What is it exactly?" Xi demanded from behind me.

Ignoring her crossness, I summoned the shadows, quickly scribbling a hasty note upon parchment, and tossing it back into the void. The message was simple, straightforward, and lacked any flattery or sincere, heartfelt proclamations to Lady Eve of the Night Court. "I don't know and that is what bothers me. I am hoping my mother will have some answers but we won't have them in time for these poor creatures. We must get moving, reaching Lacail is of great importance and we must hurry. I have a feeling the town will not be very safe for much longer."

Xi sighed, "You think the seal is in Lacail, don't you?"

I watched the trolls with sadness in my eyes for the decision I would have to make here today. Whatever this power was, it was not their fault but they would pay the price. "I do."

A warm hand encased my shoulder and I dragged my eyes from the ridiculous yet sad scene and into sincere hazel ones. "I know you do not want to harm them, General, but whatever this power is, they are already suffering, at this point killing them is a mercy."

Reaching across, I placed my hand on Riley's, patting it gently. "I know. Please keep the air around them, without it the shadows cannot do their task, and if they cannot then their deaths will not be swift and painless."

He grunted, dropping his hand. "I can do it if you need me to, General. It can be as if they are falling asleep."

I shook my head. "No my friend, I'd rather not have the bloodshed of the innocent be on your hands." Dropping my voice low, I added, "You've had enough of that already."

He nodded, searching my gaze and seeing in them my understanding and acceptance of his past. Riley Dragoon would never need to convince me why he had done what he had—because I would have done the same.

"Keep the air around them please." I exhaled harshly, waving to the shadows and watching them open wide their monstrous jaws of darkness. The troll's angry roars and fearful screeches were muffled but I could see the glint of fear of their impending doom in their feral red eyes. The herd of camphor had since disappeared into the sparkling Lac Asrai, seeking refuge beneath the surface while the shadows snapped shut around Riley's air prison, silencing the trolls forever.

"Goddess," Xi whispered, "that was just as fucking terrifying as the last time and it's just trolls."

"Not helping Xi," Riley hissed over his shoulder.

Biting the inside of my cheek until I felt the sharp pain of the soft flesh breaking and tasted blood seeping into my mouth, I turned away towards the jungle. "No need to defend me or them, Riley. I know what I am and so do the shadows. I deal in death and they relish in making a terrifying show of it."

"You may deal in death, Remnant Dark, but you are not immune to the pain it causes. How many times do you bleed inside when you take a life?"

Startled, I looked up at him in shock. "Enough that the scars are so thick that I barely feel it anymore," I replied honestly, watching as the shadows slimmed, floating up to me gracefully. "Well done my loves. Now go, send word to my mother, give her the note and await her answer before you return."

The shadows popped out of existence, and I swallowed hard against the bitter sadness welling inside and the sharp metallic taste of blood in my mouth.

Tilting my head up to the warmth of the sun, I breathed in deep. Its rays most assuredly mocked me this time, for its gentle heat had no effect on the chill that laid a new layer of ice upon my heart.

This was who I was and who I would always be. There were no tears that could thaw this frost and no light that could possibly live within my darkness.

Plastering on a look of indifference, I turned to the weary elementals silently watching me. "Let us hope the rest of our travels are uneventful."

Both of them snorted in unison and I smiled, feeling lighter just in their presence.

Chapter 14

NEVER IN ALL THE goddess's dreams and wishes would I have ever expected to see the most deadly fae living amongst us mourn over trolls. But she did, her dark hair blew gently with the comforting breeze, the sun poured over her figure to chase the darkness, and the lapping waves stretched towards her to wash away the sadness. From where she stood, her bitter grief soaked into the earth, I did not need to see her face, nor hear her and Riley's exchange to know that her decision had caused her great anguish.

I swallowed down the solemn heaviness upon the air, my emotions still reeling from the loss of the tunnels, the dark secrets Riley harbored, and even more so from the bright flame of his declared love for me. *Everything* about Riley Dragoon felt like he was mine and I was his but still I said...no. I denied my heart the one thing it always wanted and as such, it shattered like glass upon stone, and I wasn't sure if we would ever be able to pick up the pieces.

When Remnant moved towards the jungle, I halted her with an outstretched hand. "Wait," I commanded, wincing at my tone.

Her brows rose at my audacity, before gazing steadily down at her arm where my hand gripped her.

Slowly, I released the smooth, pale skin etched with black ink. "Please wait, I'd like to..." I looked up at Riley out of instinct, his mouth twitching with a small, knowing smile despite our discourse. Damn it to fucking Faerie and back, that fae loved it when I went soft but I had no goddess damn time for it. My softness was beaten out of me as a faeling. The rigorous training and lonely nights locked in a dungeon to see how long I could withstand *their* torture was enough to make any fae harden to stone. It was either that or break. My parents held very little sympathy or remorse when I did break for it was all part of my training, skills I needed to survive in this world, traits I needed to become unrivaled. If I did not bleed enough, if I was not quiet enough, if I did not stay conscious long enough, then I was not powerful enough and the torture would begin anew. I would have to endure it all again, each day a new routine, always finding more and more sadistic ways to *train* me, to *improve* me.

I was my parents' prodigy, even if my eye color was a blasphemy upon their name. With the seraphic beauty of my mother, the might of my father, and the combined power of our family's legacy to wield firestone, I would make up for it above all else to carry on the good and regal name of Chin.

Fuck that. If I could strip my name from my soul I would. But for the fae, names held power and even I still believed them to be sacred, even if it had come from *them*.

An emerald gaze gave me another pointed look.

Scowling, I sighed exasperatedly, "Before we leave, I'd like to pay my respects to the trolls. You are right, they were innocent in all of this and I would like to honor that."

The shadow fae general's stare took on that of bright curiosity, the sadness suddenly morphing into gratitude. "Of course, if that is what you wish."

I nodded, shooting Riley an annoyed glance at his knowing smile and the pride in his eyes. Rolling my own, I strolled to just a few feet from the water's edge. Breathing deep, I summoned the earth, knowing exactly how I wanted to honor the trolls who perished upon these shores. Churning beneath the lac's surface, there was rich sediment, full of minerals of calcium, magnesium, and even iron. Diffusing the sediment from the water, I filled six perfect spheres, for six imperfect trolls, with the precious composites of citrine—a stone that no fae would be able to ignore and not pay reverence to. We were often caught by its soothing power to comfort the harsh savage within. We were but cultured monsters after all.

Pulling my creation from Lac Asrai, the stone swirled around the precious crystals, sealing them inside before I lowered them upon the watery shore. The soft waves welcomed each stone with a gentle caress of its glittering waters. Small splits within the large round boulders, the height of an average fae, revealed the warm golden and orange glow of the citrine crystals within. Shifting them until they were laid perfectly in a staggered row, they would be a sight to behold for anyone who ever passed these shores.

"They are called *moeraki*," I said softly, trying to ignore the wondrous stares directed my way. I hid more of my face with my hair, their awe-struck gazes making me uncomfortable. "The fae of Faerie may not know why these *morekai* have been placed but they will not be able to pass without honoring them. The citrine inside will influence peace and healing should any choose to stay awhile."

"*Morekai*, a place to sleep during the day," Remnant breathed, her smile wide with gratitude that beamed on her beautiful face. "A perfect way to honor our troll brethren."

I grunted and inhaled sharply when suddenly her dark beauty was wrapped around me in a strong hug, her tattooed arms squeezing me tightly.

Riley choked on a laugh when I gave him a horrified look over her shoulder imploring him to save me. Surely he wouldn't leave me in her arms, even as furious as I was with him.

"Thank you, Xi Chin," she whispered.

Patting her back awkwardly, I stammered, "Yeah...ummm don't mention it. Please."

She pulled away just as quickly and set a respectable distance between us before swiping back her dark hair. Passing one last lingering look on the *moeraki* boulders behind me, she turned without looking back, her stride confident and swift. "We can linger no longer, we must get moving into the Saltu if we are to reach Lacail in time."

"Into the Saltu? Are you serious?" Ancient fae for jungle—the Saltu was where fae disappeared and never came back, no doubt caused by the Faerie rings hidden deep within and also because of its borders with the spirit realm of The Veil. The elementals of the plains knew this and avoided it at all cost. I wasn't about to go anywhere near that place.

The stillness of the air and lack of sunlight within the jungle had every instinct of mine on high alert. I never even dared to tunnel under the damn thing because of its ancient roots that seemed to stretch to Sheol itself. As a fae prone to survival, I was not about to disturb the death god even if the challenge of it did make me more than curious to try.

Cocking her hand on her hip, Remnant pursed her lips. "What would you suggest then?"

"Not risking death and avoiding the anthousai as much as possible," I said dryly, suppressing the shudder brought on by just thinking about the flower nymphs of the rings. Their siren abilities coaxed even the strongest of minds into their realm. They stole your pleasure and your vitality until you were nothing but dancing bones. "Follow the lac's edge until we reach the plains."

Remnant looked beyond my shoulder wrinkling her nose. "We would lose a whole day taking that route, besides I'd rather stay away from the water."

"You were more than happy to swim in it a few moments ago," I snapped.

She grinned. "It's not the lac that worries me, it's the waterways."

Riley grunted with understanding, his tone suspicious. "You are concerned about the water fae again? What role do they play in all of this?"

Remnant sighed, "Hopefully none at all, goddess willing." Shaking her head, she turned back to the woods. "No, we can't waste time and this is the fastest way. Through the Saltu we must go." Winking over her shoulder, her green eyes glittered. "Don't worry Xi, I will protect you." She laughed as she disappeared into the dense foliage.

"Did you hear that? There's that tone again, Ri." I glared at him, pointing in the shadow fae's direction accusingly, not missing her quiet chuckling from within the jungle.

Riley snorted, shaking his head. "I am starting to think there is no better sound in the world," leaning into me, his voice dropped low, "Aside from your gasps of pleasure, terrella."

I inhaled sharply, falling into those mischievous hazel eyes despite myself, and relishing in the soft whisper of air stroking sensually across my body.

His lips curled into a satisfied smile, before he started to gently guide me towards the jungle, "That's it, terrella, that's the sound. The most perfect one in this entire universe."

Brushing him off, I sent him a scathing look. "You will not hear it from me again then. Not until I have my answers from you."

His eyes that were bright with humor and desire, quickly saddened. "I know, goddess I know. When there is time you can tear all the answers you wish from my soul but please know that what I did in my past was not for power, Xi, it was for love."

My mouth opened but no words escaped. My mind may have betrayed me but thankfully my feet did not as I made a hasty retreat straight into the Saltu.

CHAPTER 15

"**G**ODDESS DAMN IT RI! I blame you for this and the general. Her tone means death, and we marched right into it!" Xi screamed as we ran through the woods, ducking and weaving frantically as tiny darts flew through the air.

Gnomes were always a pain in the ass but these ones were goddess damn feral. Hissing and screeching, angered beyond reasoning, they had been chasing us through this jungle for far too long. All because I just happened to piss on their nesting grounds...how the Sheol was I supposed to know that?

"Fuck! Xi jump!" I snarled back, weaving air to launch her high above into the canopy, narrowly avoiding the large faerie ring that she was about to fall headlong into.

Without pausing to check on her, I continued to roll and dodge, cutting through the thick forest as quickly as I could. Anything to outrun those possessed gnome bastards. Somewhere behind me, peals of exhilarated laughter chimed from Remnant

Dark. I failed to see the fucking amusement but I sure as goddess wasn't going to look back, unless I wanted a dart stuck in my eyeball.

"Poisonous darts incoming again!" Remnant shouted, bringing up our rear.

I did not hesitate when cool shadows fell heavily over my shoulders and draped down my back just moments before a volley of darts whistled through the air. More than several whizzed by and I cursed as the plant life instantly blackened from the poisonous weaponry. "Fucking goddess," I cursed, jumping over the dead plants, not even willing to chance that the poison was no longer active.

Xi hissed with vexation in front of us, swinging and jumping from branch to branch, her strong athletic build demonstrating power and finesse that was more than pleasing to watch. Though the image was ruined by the five needle-biting bastards hot on her heels, their beards sticky with sap and drool from their hunger to hunt.

Flinging air outwards, I knocked them all off balance, hearing their howls and screeches all the way until they hit the ground below.

When the earth began to tremble, echoing Xi's frustrations, I knew her control on her power was slipping. That *vibe* was back...I wasn't even sure if it had fucking left. Gritting my teeth, I mentally shoved away her damning words and the distrust on her end that was only growing with each leg of this journey.

Dancing away, the earth split like a bursting dam, and with it a sense of dread shivered up my spine. If it wasn't for Remnant not wanting to hurt these little gnome bastards, our powers combined would have ended them quickly. Instead we were running for our lives and this shit was about to get much, much worse.

"Xi don't!" I hollered, seeing ahead where splintering earth was rapidly racing toward another Faerie ring sitting peacefully in the jungle—but it was too late. "Ah goddess," I whispered, stumbling to a stop when the earth violently shattered the wide circular ring of brightly glowing flowers, breaking the containment that held back something far more sinister than gnomes.

Remnant came to a sliding halt next to me along with the flower pissing bastards. Paralyzed with terror, the bearded savages stared at the broken ring briefly before shrieking in panic, turning tail and running back to wherever they goddess damn came from, as if they had never bothered to chase us for hours in the first place. Back to their daily life of pee pollination and farting out glitter.

"Well this can't be good," Remnant mused and I raised a brow at her, admiring her attempted note of levity and also the fact that she was not even breathing heavily.

I snorted, brushing my hair from my sweaty brow before unsheathing my scimitars. "I really wish you hadn't said that." With a quick toss, I launched one of my swords into the air as Xi dropped from the trees, landing in a crouch before catching the blade. Standing, she expertly twirled the scimitar in a series of whirling silver form that normally would have made my dick as hard as stone if it wasn't for the white mist oozing out from the cursed broken Faerie ring.

Xi's cheeks puffed before she exhaled forcefully, her white hair briefly flying from her face. "Maybe it won't be that bad."

My other brow quirked, this time at her. "Are you goddess damn serious right now?" As if on cue, a long wailing cry cut the still jungle air, blasting the white mist into an eruption of dense, white fog, blocking out our sight. "You just had to say it, didn't you?" I muttered, reaching outward blindly to where I had last seen Xi, no longer able to see her beauty but still feeling her warmth.

Pulling her into me, I dragged us both to a very perplexed shadow fae who was watching her dormant shadows flicker in and out around her forearms before disappearing.

"Tell me that's not what I think it is?" I hissed, dreading the answer I already knew.

"Well it's definitely not good, and likely very, very bad," she mused, shaking her head.

"How is stating the obvious by any means helpful? What is happening? Where have the shadows gone and better yet, why haven't the other ones come back?" Xi snarled back. I groaned, pinching the bridge of my nose while the two females glared at one another. I was in the worst possible position for this and in normal self preservation mode I would have taken more than a few steps back from this face off.

But this shit wasn't normal. Something was off...missing, I could *feel* it.

Hard emerald eyes cutting through the opaque mist narrowed on Xi and I shifted uncomfortably at their intensity. "Our powers have become void in this mist—a mist that is normally contained within the Faerie rings. It is how the anthousai are so powerful once you are trapped within the rings."

"Impossible," Xi breathed.

Dark hair fell over her shoulder when she tilted her head, the long strands disappearing in the dense fog. "Go on then, both of you. See if you can harness either one of your elements?"

Breathing deep and keeping contact with Xi, I attempted to latch onto the air. All it would take was one forceful gust to rid us of this entire debacle, but when I reached for my power I found nothing. Just pure emptiness. This was what was missing.

"Nothing," I divulged, looking down at Xi to see her shaking her head at me, lips pressed tightly, her singular grey eye wide with alarm. Sighing, I tapped my sword held tightly in her hand, my tone confident. "Then old school it is, just cleverness and steel. What could go wrong with that?"

"Indeed, Ri, what could possibly go wrong?" Remnant mused. Her sarcasm not lost on me. Sighing, she quickly stripped off her leather vest, pushing it up and over her head, baring her torso and causing me to damn near fall over—never mind the fact that she had just called me Ri.

Darting a quick glance down at Xi whose mouth also hung open, we watched as the General's creamy, perky breasts swayed and her firm cut abs rippled as she stooped for a knife at her boot. Flashes of silver and the sound of furious shearing of cut leather had her spinning towards us soon after.

Braided from the strips of her clothing, Remnant held up several leather bindings. I jerked back, crashing into Xi when the shadow fae stepped towards me, unsure what the Faerie fuck she was up to. Anticipating my reaction, Remnant's strong hand snapped out, faster than I had ever seen anyone move before, and gripped my belt dragging me closer.

I cleared my throat, averting my eyes to not stare down at the full breasts that were just short of my torso, as she began to tie the makeshift leather rope to me without permission. "I uh...I'm not sure what is going on here and I mean no offense General but I am not seeking—" a sharp jerk of the knot she was cinching crashed my body into hers. Her firm, petite frame radiated a hot heat through my clothing but when my eyes looked down into hers, all I saw was an impish smile.

Thoroughly confused, I glanced over at Xi for assistance, but she seemed to have recovered much quicker than I had. Giving me the first full grin since she found out about my power, Xi nodded. "Go on Ri...what are you not seeking?"

"You are goddess fucking serious right now?"

Remnant snickered, reaching up to pat my cheek. "Do not worry Dragoon, I am not tying you up to have my wicked way with you. I'll leave that to our lovely Xi." Tossing a leather cord to Xi, she stepped away from me winking.

Licking my lips I watched them both warily, even more confused when Xi began to tie her own binding to her belt, "What order would you have us in?" Xi said as she tugged on the rope, testing her knot, and peering at Remnant through the dense fog.

Still not knowing what the goddess was happening, I glanced between them, trying desperately not to stare at the beautiful, bare body that was Remnant Dark and feeling like a fool at the way Xi was watching me do so.

"Best to keep Ri in the middle. If we come across the anthousai they will be more interested in him. He already looks like a flower nymph with his green hair and eyes the color of the woodlands."

"I do not—wait, what in the Sheol is going on." Having enough of the play, I folded my arms across my chest, glaring at both of their smirking faces. Not tits. Faces. Goddess help me.

More soft snickers were my only answer before Xi tugged me into her. Stumbling, I reeled on the balls of my feet, bowing over her body to stop from crushing her with my full weight while she simply winked up at me and planted a kiss upon my mouth. Effectively cutting off my words of outrage.

"Don't worry my little flower nymph, we will take such good care of you," she purred up at me.

Looking between us and watching her tie her binding to mine, the pieces finally clicked together inside my addled brain. This was for safety...not for some kinky sex in the middle of a threatening mist with the female of my dreams and another of nightmares.

I goddess damn needed more male friends.

Another jerk, had me looking down at the source, Remnant now binding us together, looping the leather around her own belt. Her exposed pale skin melded into the mist that was already thickening. "We need to stick together," she explained. "To be separated will be offering our lives to the death god in this mist. No games, no tricks. Just straight to the pits of Sheol or in a land of no mercy in the Faerie rings. I'm not ready for either. Are you?"

I huffed, waving at the leather cord between us. "You could have just said that from the beginning and why not ask me to use my shirt, it would have given us more room should we need to fight while still being anchored together."

Her dark head shook, the details of her face fading. "Leather is much harder to sever, the cloth of your pretty shirt would be too frail. I could have used your pants, they are longer and also leather but I thought you'd rather not have your swinging balls exposed in a jungle of gnomes and the siren-like revelry of the flower nymphs. Then, there was the decision of my own or Xi's pants to use. And we both know one would have deemed you helpless because if you had a bare pussy and fine ass to look at..." She shrugged, indicating the rest did not need to be said.

I choked, fucking *choked* before blurting, "Do you—fuck, do you at least want my shirt?"

Xi chortled behind me, patting my back in sympathy as I stammered like a damn faeling.

Remnant's eyes glowed through the mist. "Nah, that would defeat the second purpose of using my shirt."

"Which is what exactly?" Feeling far too foolish at this point to assume I knew anything that was going on in Remnant Dark's head.

She smiled. "To stay cool of course. It's hotter than the goddess's tits out here. What other reason is there?"

I shook my head, sighing with a reluctant smile. "What else indeed."

CHAPTER 16

Remnant

BEADS OF SWEAT TRAILED the length of my bare back. Crouched low in the thick white mist, I studied the moss upon the trees. Without the sunlight, the sight of stars, or even the prevailing winds, we walked blindly through the stagnant and quiet Saltu. The silence of the jungle was eerie and damning, like the stillness before a violent storm. For the past hour, the sense of being watched prickled on my skin, now permanent, the instinct to run like a hunted animal was fierce—but I was no prey.

"We are still going in the right direction," I whispered, feeling Xi and Riley searching for me through the now solid white fog.

"Faerie fantastic," Xi muttered.

A twig snapped in the distance but it may as well have been a bomb exploding, deafening in its aftermath. "Well we just went from fantastic to terrific," I whispered, peering into the mist towards the sound.

"Please tell me that's just pissing gnomes and not the anthou-sai," Riley breathed, leaning towards the sound moving around us, his firm chest brushing against my bare shoulder.

Pulling a pair of daggers from my boot, I relished the cool steel clamped in my sweaty hands. "The fae cannot lie, they are here." I pursed my lips, if we stayed here to fight we would have no chance, not with this dense jungle but if I could get us to a clearing then perhaps we could survive. "Have any of you ever seen ant pairs run?" I questioned, staring into the thick fog still tracking the sounds.

I could feel Riley grin despite his alert state radiating through the ties that bound us, "Sorry to disappoint, General, but watching ants is not one of my favorite pastimes."

Xi snorted softly, "While my partner is quite imperceptive today, I understand your meaning, a tandem run. Total unison."

Riley chuckled roguishly, "You mean a fuck run."

I wiped away the sweat now pebbling on my brow, my chest tight from the thick air clogging my lungs. "If that analogy helps you," I laughed quietly. "I've seen you two move, I have no doubt you could do it on your own but now I need to know if you can follow me. My movement, my direction, my coordination. If we are to survive this then we must not get separated and we must work together. No more hesitations, no more doubts, you are committed wholly to me. If you can do that—then *nothing* will ever stop me from ensuring your survival."

And for what-ever else the damned future would bring, my mind whispered.

Voices singing soft melodies began to float on the foggy mist, and with it the sweet combined smell of lilac, berries, and roses. Soft titillating giggles joined their seductive song, the delicate tones cutting through the dense air.

"I await your answers."

Riley's response was immediate, feeling what I already had since the first moment I laid eyes on them. This was more than just a quest, it was the turning point of destiny. "We are with you, General."

"For now," added Xi, hesitation still in her voice.

I winked into the mist towards her. "Good enough for me, I hope you can run and hold your breath."

Facing forward, I launched us deep into the mist, our bind-ings staying slack, as if I were running alone, and I smiled. We were one, a harmonious extension of myself just like my shadows, racing in tandem away from the sweet song and seductive giggles.

"Duck," I commanded through gritted teeth bowing under a low branch, catching the damp moss in my periphery. "Right," I breathed. Dodging, I felt them both veer with me. A wide smile spread across my face despite the grimness of our situation and the song growing stronger around us. Goddess, I hadn't felt this synchronous with another in so long. Even then it was just my brother and I that could move this way. To be this connected to two fae I had just met was surreal, euphoric, a goddess damn blessing and I prayed, oh did I pray as our feet hit the jungle floor together that they would choose to stay with me. I needed them to stay with me. I could not do this alone. Not anymore. "Jump."

Together we leapt through the white mists and I closed my eyes, enjoying the brief moment of freedom. Freedom from the constant vigilance of having to watch my back within a treacherous court and the lethal games they played. All because of two elemental fae, that even now still planned to usurp the very throne I served.

My life was always full of goddess damn ironies.

"Swords," I barked, catching sight of long trailing starburst blooms of blues and pinks. I didn't flinch at the dual hiss of steel at my back, and with daggers already in my hands, we landed softly within a clearing.

Giggles surrounded us, flashes of their flower petal hair weaved in and out of this mist, and I raised my blades the moment their teasing coo's began.

"Little, little, shadow."

My blood froze. Recognizing the taunt and the voices.

More laughter, "Little shadow is not so little anymore."

More melodious chatter, "Little, little, shadow must have missed us."

"They know you?" snarled Xi.

Clenching my teeth, I peered into the mist following their teasing songs. "When I was young, I fell into their rings." Narrowing my eyes, "How many do you count, Ri?" I knew he had been keenly tracking them. A whisperer of air, his ability to track the smallest of sounds was impeccable—a skill my research informed me of.

"Five," Riley breathed, raising his sword up high.

"Agreed," I nodded, my daggers mirroring his sword.

"One, two, three, four, five, once I caught a fae alive," cooed a voice behind us, her voice bouncing as if she were skipping at our backs.

Another giggle to our front, "Oh yes, sister, I want to play! Six, seven, eight, nine, ten, then I caught their little friends."

Clapping and chortles echoed, "Yes, yes, let's play. Why did you catch them so," called out another.

"Because I could not let them go."

My eyes darted to my left, just barely making out the slender silhouette of a flower nymph. A green body, layered silver bark skin upon her face, starburst blooms like that of hyacinth fluttering around wide eyes that were the color of the glowing sun, disappeared into the mist from whence she came.

"Goddess," Xi breathed, bringing her sword to her face. "They are playing with us."

Riley groaned, "To what purpose?"

My lips thinned, scanning the white fog, poised and ready. I yearned for my shadows to return but even they likely could not penetrate this kind of fog. It nulled all power... when I had fallen into the rings as a young faeling they could not assist me then and I felt their absence just as keenly now.

More salacious laughter and then a strong humming vibrated the mist, caressing over my skin with a horrifyingly lulling pleasantness that took much for me to resist.

"What did you do with them?" purred another, continuing their taunting song. Her voice whispered against my ear but when I turned towards her she was gone, leaving only a trailing sound of amused giggles.

"Made them dance until their end," they all hissed in unison, stepping out of the mist together like perfectly cultivated flowers in a garden. An array of pinks and blues, whites and purples, their bodies flowed like willows dancing in the wind. Green naked skin glistened in the mist, offsetting their petal hair and their encased masked faces of silver bark.

They were beautiful—and by the brilliant sunny glow in their eyes, they were *hungry*.

"I don't dance without a partner...unless you're asking to be mine, anthousai." I stepped forward, blades still high, the beads of sweat trailing down my naked skin forcing a shiver from me just as much as their lingering, voracious eyes.

I was a distraction, a weapon, and simultaneously, without a tug on our bonds, Riley and Xi fell fluidly in line at my back—the warriors that would wield me. And like a good blade and shield, I would make sure this was where the anthousai greeted death. Afterall, Sheol needed more souls to satisfy its god.

CHAPTER 17

I SAW NOTHING, ASIDE from the faint outline of Riley's wide shoulders, and the slightest hue of his wavy green hair that even now, my traitorous fingers ached to run through. The thick fog was everywhere, and my lungs burned from my sorry attempt to keep the seductive fragrance of the anthousai from compelling me into their revelry. Oxygen deprived, my sword arm shook, straining to hold my blade and the slick of sweat coating my palms made my grip even more challenging.

All made worse by their creepy as fucking Faerie nursery song of doom.

Between us, as a half naked shield, Remnant Dark faced the nymphs head on. "You've had your fun, now it's time to return to your circle," the general called out. The hard edge of her tone made me shiver, flashbacks of the night of The Wailing suddenly dominant in my mind. This was no longer the fae that talked to birds and shadows, nor was it the one that our world honored with its elements, this was the fae of death...one that was at the center of all my night terrors for the past six months.

Ignoring the eerie allure of laughter and the tension in the air, I focused on Riley's strong silhouette, my scimitar raised out to the side, mirroring his powerful stance. Poised and ready, a warrior through and through, I had yet to see someone match his savage ways on the battlefield aside from Remnant Dark.

A curse, a harsh breath, then we moved. A slow dance along the open clearing. Closing my eyes, I felt them both like I did the energy of the earth, the flow of their bodies, the hiss of Riley's steel slashing outward, mine following simultaneously with it.

The sharp cry when my blade made contact with a solid being brought a satisfied smile to my face, but the moment was brief and my slight pause fatal. The cord between us grew taut, the leather groaning, and I slid towards Riley blindly just seconds before I heard his soft grunt and the tearing clothing. My blood froze at his sharp inhale. I didn't need to see through the thick fog to know Ri had been hit, and it was more than just a graze. Furious, my sight caught the curvy shape of willowy legs peeking through the mist, and I reacted. Sweeping low, my scimitar whistled, my weakened state forgotten as I put power into my slice, cutting clearly through the retreating nymph that dared to harm my air elemental.

My air elemental...fucking goddess, my chest tightening from an aching heart. How was I ever going to walk away from him once he explained his past?

Hot blood sprayed across my face, and I grinned ferally, latching onto the euphoric satisfaction of my vengeance rather than my impending loss of the fae I loved. The nymph's following scream was shrill and I relished the sound—anything was better than their singing.

Crumbling at my feet, the anthousai writhed on the ground, her legs cut cleanly from her body, she wept and pleaded for help. Raising my blade high to end her pathetic existence, bright yellow eyes snapped up to meet my fury, and I forgot not to breathe. Sweet scented pheromones enveloped me in a cloud, and every part of my body spasmed to a tension driven stall, seized by the anthousai's power. Panting, I fought against the invisible restraint but it only served to drown me more in the haze of her wonderful scent.

"Xi," she whispered sweetly, "oh Xi, heal me, don't let me die. You don't *really* want to kill me. All you need to do is cut the cord and heal me." Her silver barked lip quivered as her green body crawled towards me, and I found myself drawn towards her, entranced.

Through hooded eyes, my resolve wavered. I didn't want to kill her, did I? I could try to heal her mangled body after all. It was my secondary power. I could heal.

"Cut the cord Xi, heal me please...heal me terrella. Please." Leaning in, deeply inhaling her lilac and berry scent, I collected the tears that spilled from the crinkles of her silver bark. The wetness spreading across my fingertips was euphoric. Cooling yet warm, it was a whispered caress with promises of love.

I heard a faint roar and someone shouting my name between the nymph's pleas, but it was something that I could not be bothered with. *She* was the most important thing in this world and she needed me. For once in my life someone *needed* me. Flipping my blade, I cut the leather in one fluid downward stroke and placed my hand on the being, willing my power to heal her.

A soft encouraging laugh, "Well done, terrella." The anthousai cooed, sitting up, her legs regenerating before me. I looked up at her, sudden clarity of what I had done hitting me in a torrent of panic before her scent engulfed me again, pulling me back under her seductive spell. "Your power doesn't work here sweet, beautiful Xi Chin and now you are mine."

"You—you healed yourself," I slurred, fighting the haze pulling me under. My tone more reverent than accusing.

Crushing me into her lush green skin, the contact sent warm tingling throughout my entire body, the brush of her fingers to draw back my hair searing me with her sadistic love. "Oh beautiful Xi, of course I can heal. Now I am going to take you away from here. Keep you safe, make sure you are loved and cared for. Wouldn't you like that, my sweet, sweet terrella?" She stroked my head, pulling me easily to my feet, and lacing our fingers intimately together.

"But—"

Her lips pressed against mine, swallowing my protesting words, and I fell into her touch. It didn't matter any more, not when her lips, smooth and hard, like polished wood nuzzled mine. A long tongue licked along the seam of my mouth and I inhaled again, desperately eager for more of her floral scent that would spiral me into exhilarating pleasure. I craved to reciprocate, to give back what she has so selflessly gifted me, my need bordering on desperation.

Lunging for her mouth I met her seeking tongue with my own, pressing myself closer to this bewitching creature who I needed more of—so badly needed more of.

I whimpered when she pulled away but she simply laughed, walking backwards, naked hips swaying, drawing me into the mist where others waited. As one they began to dance around us, laughing and twirling, circling like the sirens of the woods that they were.

"Oh how lovely, Clarissa," one crooned.

"She's perfect, worth the loss of our sister to obtain," giggled another and I groaned, veering into her stroking touch.

I *needed* more.

"Please," I whispered, not knowing what I was begging for but knowing only they could give it to me.

"And ever so willing," purred another, "You were right Elaie, this one is perfect for us. Won't you dance with us, my love?"

Different hands pulled me, touching me everywhere. Guiding me into a sway and then a heady rhythm. My body burned, sweat soaked my skin, and my core throbbed, wanting more than just seductive touches and sweet whispers. Laughter rang in my ears and the last bit of warning in the back of my mind disappeared as I threw my head back and joined their taunting giggles.

Expelled from my mind, the last of my inhibitions disappeared like the precious air that I no longer needed, forgetting why it was so very precious to begin with.

CHAPTER 18

Tʜᴇ sᴇᴠᴇʀᴇᴅ ᴄᴏʀᴅ ꜰᴇʟʟ in slow motion through the fog, swaying to brush softly against my leg and it was everything my nightmares were made of. Pure terror and heart stopping loss had me lunging straight into the mist with nothing but desperate fear. My outstretched arms quivered, futile in their search through the vacant air, suddenly a reflection of the vacuous chasm that my heart was falling into.

"They took her," I roared, wildly sweeping through the fog, stumbling blindly in a circle, restricted by the taut leather cord that still connected me to Remnant. Seized in a chokehold, horror rippled through my body when the white mist began to withdraw with no Xi in sight—not a whisper of her remained in the clearing of the dark, dense jungle.

Remnant's head snapped up from her query, her lips pulled back in a viscous snarl. Still holding a slain nymph in her arms, she threw the sadistic creature to the side, her dagger sliding from its body in a sickening yet satisfying spray of blood. The gore dripped down the front of her bare chest but she paid it no heed, instead, she grabbed my arm in a rush, chasing after the quickly retreating mist. "Come on Ri," she cried, dragging my stunned, grief-stricken frame. "We need to follow the mist or we will lose her forever!"

Half stumbling, half running I stared blindly at her bloodied hand wrapped around my arm pulling me along.

Lose her forever...

"Fucking Faerie," Remnant spat at the retreating mist that seemed to disappear faster than we could run.

Lose her forever...

Crashing to a halt, the last deposit of the ghostly fog disappeared, leaving us surrounded by nothing but tropical greens, suspicious looking flowers, and hot, stagnant air.

Releasing a slew of curses, Remnant sliced the cord between us and I winced, the leather swaying just like its twin moments ago when Xi was lost. Pacing, the jungle floor crunched beneath the general's stomping feet while she ripped her tight ponytail from its tie with another round of colorful swearing. Tugging her fingers through her long strands, I could see the dark, wet, shine of nymph blood soiling her silky locks.

Xi hated it when blood got in her hair. It stained her luscious white hair pink for weeks and she would complain non-stop until it was finally purged from those pure strands that I loved to tuck behind her ear.

I swallowed hard, wondering if I would ever feel it between my fingers again.

"We need to find a Faerie ring," the shadow fae muttered, studying the trees in front of her, the dark, dormant shadows, returning since the mist had retreated, rapidly flickering around her body. "But how are we going to know which one is the right one?"

Like the echo from the end of a tunnel, her muttered pondering blurred to an indistinct hum. Blinking long and slow, my world came crashing down around me, and I stared into the endless green, a bottomless pit of never-ending despair.

"Shit, Ri," emerald eyes blazed only inches from mine, Remnant's dark brows scrunched together with alarm. How long had she been standing there? "We are going to figure this out," she said softly, her blood-stained hand reaching up to cup my face, "I need you to focus though. Can you do that for me, Dragoon? Now is not the time to shut down. We need to act quickly, time is fickle in the Faerie rings."

Time is fickle.

My lips pulled back in a sneer—time was more than just that, it was a fucking illusion that always took and never gave back. A countdown that could easily be filled with regrets if one was not careful and that was all I felt right now. Fucking regret for wasting what I once had.

She sighed, attempting to pull her hand away after seeing the flash of anger in my eyes, but I stopped her with a harsh and desperate grip, digging my fingertips into her pale, tattooed skin. "You have been inside the rings?"

Her bare chest heaved with a deep sigh, the blood that had splattered on her dry and flaking as she ignored my handle on her body. "Unfortunately."

I squeezed her arm harder, my grip punishing but she never once winced. Instead, her eyes softened, empathy and worry for me shining in their emerald depths. I did not deserve such worry and I was past caring how pathetic I sounded. "How?" I choked, "How did you get out?"

"I didn't, my mother did. A fae must stand judgement to break the hold of a Faerie ring and then must be strong enough to pull the anthousai's victims back through. But it is dangerous, Ri. It's not your actions that are judged, anyone can walk into a Faerie ring with proclamations of love but not everyone can face the truth in their own heart. If you are not deemed worthy, death will be inevitable."

I dropped her arm, my confidence returning. "Nothing is more dangerous than walking this world alone with a shattered heart and an empty soul," I growled. "Xi Chin is mine. They will not keep her," I added darkly.

Black hair spun as Remnant pivoted, first staring back into the jungle and then excitedly back at me. "That's it!" She smiled widely. "Sweet goddess that's it. You must use your power to find her."

I froze, my breath catching in the back of my throat with the same realization. Damn my soul to Sheol and back but I could not. I *would* not. Playing dense, I exhaled, "I fail to see how my air can help find a Faerie ring?"

She crossed her arms, covering her naked breasts and giving me a pointed look that reminded me of my mother when she used to scold me for whatever mischief I had caused for the day. Those memories were few and far between now, and Remnant was resurfacing them with too much ease. Memories that were too painful to even think of fully...forever tainted by the cruel fate of my mother's final days.

When the silence stretched between us, and the general's look began to burn holes into my skull, I licked at my lips, hissing between my teeth. "Fuck Rem, if you're alluding to my other power, then you know how vile it truly is, how monstrous it is. Just the small bit of Xi knowing I had used it has her already walking away from me. If I actually do open them up..." I shook my head cursing. "I'll possess her, I'll siphon her power, drain her dry, wield combined power through her, make her hurt others...with it, she is naught but a weapon or tool to use. Her free will gone—and when she finds out that not only have I used it, but used it on her, I'll lose her forever."

"I don't believe that for one goddess damn second Riley Dragoon. When she inhales, you're the only air she wants to breathe, when she touches you, you're her earth to stay grounded, when she speaks your name, you're the only ruler she will bend a knee for. It is impossible for you to ever lose her because she is so interwoven into your very essence...just as you are threaded so thoroughly through hers. Xi will always choose you, Ri, and it is not due to the influence of your power. It's because her heart chooses you, her soul chooses you. Because of that, you have been given a gift far greater than any other—a gift greater than a bond of the soul."

I blinked at the shadow fae, swallowing hard and holding back the tears of despair flooding my eyes. "How do you see all that?" I choked, "You have only known us for a few days. We have known each other for hundreds of thousands."

"Sometimes, Riley Dragoon, it is harder to see who we are under the scars that we ourselves have given power to. In time it becomes our truth, a truth that is just as blinding as any lie."

"Our truth has been blind for a long time," I sighed with resignation, lifting the severed cord and frowning at it. Fingertips brushing against the frayed leather, I snarled, crushing it in my hand and reaching down into the darkest depths of my mind where the locked power I had banished but never escaped from was hidden. Exhaling slowly, I undid the mental locks, feeling Xi's essence bloom to life, then her unique scent of fresh grass and polished stone plucked from a riverbed assaulted my senses. The thrum of her heart quickly followed, beating fast and erratic, her breath ragged, a sound I knew so well—I swallowed hard. Her pleasure hit me like a blow to my gut and rage burned through my veins. There was only one reason why Xi would be feeling pleasure in a Faerie ring and it sure as goddess wasn't by her fucking choice.

The tethered collar around her neck, one bewitched to be hidden even from her sight, hummed in welcome as I summoned it—summoned her.

Grunting, I reared back when my pull was cut off, like having a door slamming into my face. "I can't pull her from the ring," I snarled, "not with my power but I do know where she is."

Pouring more energy into the bond, I began to race in the direction of the barrier, tearing blindly through the jungle, not giving a fuck about the hissing gnomes or the dragon plants that snapped at my heels. I even ignored the shouting warnings from Remnant. None of that mattered as I rode the winds to swiftly hurtle me through the jungle.

Blasting through a wall of vines with a cyclone of air, I snarled hatefully at the floral ring in front of me. Hyacinth flowers waved softly in the remains of my winds, taunting me with their little innocent star buds.

I glared, their beauty a cruel monster, an illusion of peace in its deadly hunger. I blinked when the petals blurred. Suddenly my knees hit the ground, losing the ability to stand. I shook my head, as realization hit me. It wasn't the flowers that were blurring but my vision.

"No," I whispered out desperately, crawling towards the ring unseeing, my hands clawing into the earth when I fell again, my face meeting the ground. The ring was just inches away, I was so close...if I could just reach a little bit further.

"Riley!" Remnant's hands firmly rolled me to my side and I silently roared with fury as she pulled me further away from the ring. I started to thrash, my body seizing and jerking against her firm hold, suddenly not in control of it. Moaning, my vision blurred in an aura haze of pinks and blues, my ears rang with derisive laughter, as the merciless scent of berries and lilacs penetrated the final shred of conscious thought I had.

Chapter 19

Remnant

"Sweet goddess," I swore harshly, my hands slipping on warm slick blood, struggling to get a grip on the thrashing Riley, needing to roll him to his side where he would be safe from himself and the wound I had not noticed earlier.

Studying the long ragged slice in his side, tiny thorns could be seen embedded in the torn flesh. Oozing with pus and blood, the rancid stench of the poison released from those thorns had already rooted deep within Riley's system.

Convulsing, his body contorted in my hold, and I bit my lip hard, throwing myself against the uncontrolled seizing that was bringing him closer and closer to the Faerie ring. Grunting, I shoved him back, impressed that even while deliriously wracked with fever, his subconscious was still trying to get to the one fae that mattered more than his own life. The one fae that was inside that ring.

Except he was useless to her now.

Gripping his head and pulling it downward, I attempted to keep his airway as the tremors continued, the bright red blood on my hands smearing upon his pale skin like war paint. And he was at war, his body violently fighting off the poison but slowly losing the battle. Thankfully, if he was any less of a stronger fae he would have died already but my time to save him was rapidly ticking down at an alarming rate.

I glared at the floral ring—and if I didn't act quickly for Xi, *she would also die.*

Neither would I allow. Not ever. These fae, even if they walked away from me forever after this quest, would always fall under my protection. From the beginning, the knowledge of them fascinated me, and when we first met they had intrigued me, now even after a couple of days, they had ensnared me. I cared for them, like the beasts of this world, there would never be a day where I didn't make sure they stayed alive in this goddess damn wreck of a life. They were essential, like the sun and moons in the sky, they held purpose, and one day it would be revealed to all.

On cue, my shadows shimmered into existence, hovering just beyond my shoulder, peering past it like a curious child, perfect last minute timing as always. "It's about fucking time you showed up," I hissed more with relief than annoyance. "Did you take the scenic route on the way back?"

Swirling down my arms, their darkness soothing and cooling, I felt the soft light fabric of a linen shirt drape over my naked skin.

"My lack of clothing isn't the issue here, my loves," I said through gritted teeth, clinging onto Riley again before he flopped right into the goddess forsaken ring. "Can you keep him protected?"

Instinctually, the shadows blanketed the seizing air elemental in a soft cocoon of black, curling around him protectively, and cooling his feverish state. Riley moaned again, his green hair damp on his brow, and his features pinched with pain.

Pulling away, I sat back on my heels with a grimace, swiping my sweaty, blood stained hair from my face.

"Can you remove the thorns?" I croaked out, a cross between a question and a command, emotion tightening my throat, watching the darkness soothe the dying air elemental

The shadows shimmered around his spasming body, consciously keeping him safe while they went about their work, parting their dark blanket to reveal his ragged skin, now thorn free but still bleeding too rapidly, unable to heal like it should. Drawing my knife, I grasped the hem of my shirt, tearing strip after strip of the soft white linen until my naval and stomach were revealed. It seemed I couldn't stay dressed long enough in this goddess forsaken jungle.

Gentle and with deft precision, the shadows assisted me in wrapping the cloth around Riley's torso. Sweat dripped from my brow with each passing of the wrap, mixing with the blood that rapidly stained the white linen like spilled ink on a fresh page. "Fuck," I screamed, wiping my bloodied hands onto my leathers just enough to rip more of my shirt off, starting the process all over again. Mere minutes felt like hours as I worked, willing the blood flow to stop with just my glare alone, and when I finally tied off the last bandage, only a small spot of red revealed itself.

Sighing with relief, I dragged my gaze up to his face. Still flushed red with fever, beads of sweat bubbled on his brow, and his lips quivered with wheezing breaths. The ragged rise and fall of his chest told me he was still fighting—and so would I.

Leaning over him, I swiped his wavy, green locks from his face to kiss his sweaty temple, whispering words I prayed he could still hear. "I will get her back Ri," I said softly, "and then you both can save each other." Pointing at the shadows, I added, "Protect him... please."

Spinning on my knees towards the seemingly innocent looking flower ring, my brows drew together, I could not heal Riley Dragoon but Xi could. I knew from my research before even tracking the elementals down, that her secondary power was healing.

Breathing deep, I knelt and closed my eyes to focus on everything that was Xi Chin. A beautiful and powerful fae that had overcome abuse in a world of strict perfection and social egotism. Exhaling, I stretched my palm out, erasing any doubt. There was no room for it, Xi's life depended on it.

I did not need to open my eyes to know the moment my hand crossed the foreboding barrier of the ring, my conscious mind lurching and dragged under until I was officially straddling the world of Faerie and the veiled realm of the anthousai.

***

Shivering, the mist curled around my body, returning me to its clammy embrace, and exposing me to its sinister aura.

A soft thrumming beat came next, the urge to step to the erotic rhythm strong enough that I felt every part of my body tense with resistance. The faint laughter through the dense mist soon joined the sounds of revelry and I bit the inside of my cheek to resist taking a step further. Currently, most of my body was still on the outside of the veil, just one goddess damn step would prove fatal for us all. Lost forever.

"I have come for Xi Lanora Chin!" I bellowed out into the beckoning mist.

Like a materializing spirit, glowing yellow eyes set upon a silver barked face appeared. The curiosity of the nymphs was always something a fae could count on if used properly. Swaying her lithe green hips, petals trailing with each passing stride, she smiled at me. "Remi darling, if you missed us so much you should have stayed the first time."

Refusing to give her any satisfaction, I held back my disgust at the memory of falling into a Faerie ring as a faeling. No more than twenty years of age, the nymphs had toyed with me endlessly and it was pure training and quite a bit of cunning that kept me free from the worst of their torture. Except it wasn't just the anthousai that drained the life force from a fae, the mist was also lethal, weakening your strength, your ability to heal, your will to fight. I held on for two whole weeks before I finally succumbed. Luckily it had been enough, because shortly after, my mother was able to pull me from the ring. I'll never forget the way she looked as she entered the ring to save me—a dark savior dressed in black lace, regal despite her bright feral eyes and the snarl on her face that foretold death.

I smiled menacingly back at the anthousai who now hovered just inches from my face. "It seems that you have missed me more Elaie. You did come when summoned, although without what I asked for." I leaned towards her, my mouth barely a hair's breadth away from her smooth wooden lips. "It was foolish of you to attack me and my friends," I whispered darkly.

A thorn-tipped green hand smothered the giggle escaping her mouth, rearing back to do so, "Friends? You? You were never meant to have anything of the like, Remi darling, no one will ever truly love you for who you are." She brushed her body up against me. "Not like my sisters and I can."

I raised my brows, "Your sisterly love is most devotional or shall we say sacrificial? How loving of you to offer up Genia's life all for a new toy to add to your collection." My hand shot out and wrapped around her neck. Petals of purple and blue cascaded around us as I drew her back towards me, baring my teeth, and savoring the shocked fear in her yellow eyes. "Give me Xi Lanora Chin right now and I'll consider not sacrificing the rest of you to Sheol's gates to join your sister." Throwing her away from me, I watched her stumble with satisfaction.

The nymph steadied her footing, her sensuous green body vibrating with anger, her floral pheromones purging outward to swarm me. But instead of being enticed, the smell was bitter, rancid, just like the being beneath.

Seeing me so wholly unaffected, her thorny finger pointed sharply with rage, her face crinkling with fury. "You know the rules, shadow fae, you must be judged. If your heart does not align with saving your friend you both will be stuck here forever." Smiling, she tossed back the colorful array of her petaled hair before she started to skip gleefully, circling me like I was prey. "Something tells me the odds are more in my favor than last time." She giggled again, recovering quickly from her rage and shock. "Oh, what a treat, really quite a feat, my sisters will be so pleased, to finally have their little shadow back on her knees."

I didn't even bother tracking her while she danced around me singing her disturbing tunes, I just stared straight into the mist, finding what I needed inward. This was not a challenge of the physical self, it was one of the heart—a heart I was very good at icing over in my loneliness. "Let your judgment begin."

More eerie laughter ensued along with Elaie's singsong voice, "Name the true reason you have come to Xi Chin's aide?"

I breathed deeply, bringing forth the image of the determined resolve of Xi as she appeared year after year at the winter solstice in the City of Light. Her aura was like a guiding star shimmering in the sky. A quality I had never seen before from a fae. Knowing that whoever this fae was she was rare among our kind.

"Our world needs an example of what true beauty really is," I answered honestly and then gasped when I felt a swift powerful punch of judgement straight into my heart. Gritting my teeth, I braced against the onslaught, my stance holding strong.

The anthousai hissed when the force retreated and my lips twitched at the small win. Disappearing into the mist, she hummed, circling me until her breath was upon the shell of my ear.

"You speak of why the world needs her but why do you?"

Why did I need her?

My brows pulled together. I knew what Xi thought, that I only searched for her because of her ability to use the firestone, but that was not the only reason. I could have easily commanded her mother or father to join my search if that were the case and they would have had no choice but to complete the mission set forth by Deirdre—especially if they wanted to keep in the queen's inner circle.

So why did I seek out Xi for myself, why did I personally want her, need her, even more so than the air elemental who I knew had already pledged himself to me? I swallowed back the bitterness of my confession.

"I am lonely, and selfishly I need a friend who is just as lonely as I am."

I braced for the stabbing judgment, but this time it was a mere pinprick upon my vulnerable heart.

The anthousai wailed, realizing their plan to keep us would not come to fruition. My stomach somersaulted. We were going to get out of here. There was no other fucking option, I would not allow it.

"If she dies here today, how would you avenge her?"

I pressed my lips into a thin line. "I would finish what she started. I would destroy Fuchai and Xizi for the pain and suffering they inflicted on the little faeling she once was and the future she could have had. Free of scars, pain, and haunted memories." I turned towards the feral nymph, who was watching with murderous eyes, no longer laughing, nor dancing, nor singing, nor humming. "And then I would hunt down every Faerie ring in this world and burn them thoroughly with your greatest weakness—firestone. You will all burn, melting away into nothing under the searing hot fires of the very stone she wields. You will be ash, anthousai, the result of the fae you maliciously stole from the world—from me."

The anthousai hissed back at me. Her yellow eyes swirling with hatred and terror.

I stepped towards her, the judgment force repelling from me, my heart was true. Selfish, and at times harsh but it was pure and it was strong, and it had the capability to love beyond what any creature of this world could handle. I just wasn't sure if anyone could love it so fully and irrevocably back.

"Give her to me now. Give me Xi Chin. And know this, you frolicking, flower bitch, when it comes to my friends—my heart will always be worthy, it will never waver, and it will always, always avenge." Waving at her dismissively, I added, "Now are you willing to die here today or are you going to give me what I desire?"

CHAPTER 20

G ASPING, I COLLAPSED INTO the arms of the shadow fae general who was scrambling back away from the faerie ring, my limp body held tightly against hers.

"It's okay," Remnant breathed heavily. "It's okay Xi, I got you."

Tears brimmed in my eyes, blurring my vision as I trembled in Remnant Dark's hold. The memories of the anthousai realm leaving a smear of sickening residue upon my soul. The vestiges of what I had done, both monstrous and mortifying.

I sobbed, this time not bothering to hold back those goddess-forsaken tears. A weakness I never cared to expose to anyone but I was so damn tired of being strong but *alone*.

The shadow fae's words from the Faerie ring still echoing hollowly in my mind. *I need a friend who is just as lonely as I am.*

Remnant's arms squeezed harder, dragging us both up to sitting with a heavy sigh. "Shh, it's okay. It'll be okay—one day, I promise. The memories will fade. I promise they will fade." Her hand ran up and down my arm soothingly as she whispered, "But for now, let it out, you're safe with me, Xi."

Sniffing, I took a shaky breath, "I heard—" I choked. "I heard what you said in there..."

My head hung, unable to continue, and unable to look into her eyes. Staring at my hands shaking in my lap, I ashamedly recounted the number of times I had been spiteful and condescending towards the General. The scars of my past were so thick they blinded me from the truth. It was clear now, Remnant Ezra Solaire Dark was playing an end game that none of us could see and she was more than worthy of my loyalty and respect.

Especially after she laid her heart and soul bare to be judged...for *me*.

A gentle hand reached up and pulled my hair back over my face, and I summoned the courage to look up at the general. Frowning, she threaded her fingertips through the tangled strands, eyes focused only on her work, never meeting my shocked gaze. A small satisfied smile spread across her face, smoothing the strands one last time before her emerald eyes met mine. "There, that is better now." She sighed, pulling her legs back to scoot away, providing distance between us before speaking again. "I meant what I said in there, Xi. You are a beautiful soul and our world needs more of it but even more, so do I. I do not expect you to feel the same. Trust is a tenuous thing, once broken it scarcely returns without a cost." Reaching out, she wiped the rest of the tears from my face and I closed my eyes briefly at her gentle touch, "Which means what I have to say next is going to be difficult," she added, her tone remorseful.

Eyes snapping open, I inhaled sharply, my pulse racing from my already heightened emotions. *Riley, where was Riley?* "What is it?"

Her brows furrowed and she nodded behind me, the words I feared spilling from her lips. "It's Riley."

Gasping, I pivoted on my knees to see him lying on his side, deathly still with Remnant's shadows wrapped around him. An exposed area of darkness revealed thick bandages stained with blood, and emitting the putrid smell of decay.

"Ri!" I cried out, scrambling to his side. My hands immediately reached for him only to pause, hovering over his deathly still frame—I did not know if my touch would harm him more. "Sweet goddess," I whispered, seeing the white pallor of his skin and the dark rimmed circles around his closed eyes. Sweat had soaked his hair, plastering it to his brow while the shadows swirled around him slowly. An action that would have caused me alarm two days ago, but now I saw it for what it was.

Tenderness, care, love. They were a reflection of their master.

Remnant crouched on the other side of Riley, drawing my attention back to her, her lips pressed grimly together. "What happened to him?" I barked.

She placed a steady confident hand upon his brow with concern, something I had not been willing to do. Afraid, I was afraid. "He was injured fighting the anthousai. The thorns in their claws when embedded into their prey are poisonous."

I swallowed hard. Guilt joining my shame. Riley had been injured because of me, my lack of concentration, my emotions got in the way just as my parents had always predicted they would. "Does the poison need to just pass through his system, can he not fight it off himself with natural healing?"

Remnant's hand stroked back his green hair, her lips pursed. "I am afraid not. The poison inside of him is lethal. I have not ever seen a fae survive anthousai thorns without the assistance of a healer." Her eyes met mine expectantly.

The air stilled in my lungs and my heart thudded in my chest—the signs of hope dying just like the fae I loved along with my chances to ever tell him so. My anger at him the past few days prevented me from recognizing the truth, why I had been so hurt by the confessions of his power. I loved Riley, more than just a friend. "I cannot...I can only heal cuts, bruises, small fractured bones," my voice trailed off in a whisper. Brokenly, I added, "My ability to heal others is limited to these trivial things. I have never been able to bring someone back from the brink of death before." Looking down at Riley a strangled sob tore from me. Another round of fresh tears falling down my face, more than I had ever cried my entire immortal life. I could not save him...I was worthless just as my parents had so often told me. This was why they had trained me to not make mistakes and here I was facing the biggest mistake of my life. I practically poured this poison down his throat.

Firm hands held my shoulders and shook me gently. "Xi," a shake, "Xi Lanora Chin. You must listen to me now."

Blinking while my heart lay dead in my chest, I looked back at the fierce shadow fae general bearing down at me.

"You have been able to heal someone from the brink of death before..." Her stern voice held no argument, but I protested anyway, I did not want her false hope. Remnant shook me gently again, cutting off my words. "Yes, you have. It was yourself. You saved yourself, Xi, the night of The Wailing."

I shook my head, "No, no, that wasn't me, it was Riley. He found a healer to save me."

Remnant snorted. "The only healer Riley found that night was the one inside of you." Her hands squeezed my shoulders and I could see hardened resolve in her stare, "Xi. Riley combined his energy with your healing power and possessed it so that you would live."

My deadened heart dropped into my stomach, like a stone sinking in water. "His energy...the one of ownership, of enslavement—possession?" I shook my head, thinking back to how desperately he had wanted to explain, both in the tunnel and when we had escaped. Both times I had shut him down, fearful of the truth and what it would mean for us...together, "No Riley would never do that to me, he could never do that to me." Remnant's hold on me broke when I fell to my hands and knees, wracked with too many emotions for my own stubborn self to bear. My fingernails dug deep into the foliage and earth, willing it to soothe this pain. "He knows—he knows what my freedom means to me," I cried, gasping at air that would not fill my lungs. I did not want that air anyway, I wanted Riley's air or none at all, making his betrayal all the more excruciating.

Even when tainted, I still wanted him. I would always want him.

Tearing from the earth, my hands flung up to my neck in horror when I felt the heavy weight of a metal ring. My recognition of Riley's possession revealed the horrifying truth for all to see. A collar, enchanted to do the bidding of the one fae I trusted above any other in this world.

"I'm so sorry Xi," Remnant whispered before continuing, "you know Riley...he would never accept a life without you. He would have done anything to save you." She sighed, "I would have made the same choice if I were him, if I had experienced *all* of what he has. His love for you is fierce and reverent. You are what keeps him grounded to this world instead of being swept away by the winds. Just like you cannot live without his air, he cannot live without your gravity."

Her words bounced against the numb barrier I shielded my emotions with, something I'd done since childhood to protect myself, but one thing she said stuck out to me and I held onto it. I wanted to understand, I *needed* to understand.

If I had experienced all of what he has...

I released the collar around my neck, slowly peering at Remnant through the white strands of my hair, swallowing back the bitterness and the contempt—emotions I never thought I'd hold towards Riley Dragoon. But I didn't want him to die, no I wanted him to live so I could see in his eyes the truth of what he had done to me and then I would walk away. I needed to walk away.

Staring down at his pale face with the god of death hovering just beyond, my voice was hard, "Tell me what I need to do. How do I save him?"

CHAPTER 21

A PLEASANT WARMTH AND a soothing hum both sweet and sinful, enveloped the dream I was in, a sound I swore I had heard before. Smiling contentedly, I curled into the warmth mumbling my own thanks for its sweet abyss. It was better than where I came from. It had been hot and feverish there but at the same time freezing. My body had been wracked with violent shakes that left me aching deeply...but here, here I was pain free.

"Goddess damn it, Riley Dragoon, come back to me."

"That's it...you're doing it Xi, the poison is leaving him, the smell is less."

I frowned, *poison*? This wasn't poison nor was it smelly. This was peace, contentment—I hesitated at the string of curses. That voice, goddess fuck that voice. A huskiness that was both sensual and comforting, the coolest of breezes in fall, and I yearned for more of its lovely caress. Perhaps then I could finally rest.

"Oh no you don't, Ri. You fucking unicorn ass. You're waking up and you're going to look me in the eyes when you tell me how you stole my freedom from me." The lovely voice hissed, more like a chill this time.

Ah, a frigid brisk wind on the first bite of winter snow, and yet despite its sting I wanted this too—craved it even.

A sharp slap, a muffled snort, and then my eyes flew open as a low groan escaped my lips.

"Who in the Sheol just slapped me? And why am I a unicorn ass?" I scowled, reaching up to rub at my eyes. Chasing away my blurred vision, I opened them again to reveal the jungle canopy above where brightly colored wisps danced among the branches and dust-glittering butterflies fluttered through the leaves. "What is that awful smell? Please tell me a gnome didn't piss on my face," I rubbed my eyes again.

"It's the poison I purged from your body, Riley Dragoon," Xi snapped at my side. A slight groan emanated from the shadow fae general on my other side.

I sat up quickly, dizziness swirling in my vision, my body wavering and weak as I struggled to stay upright with a curse.

"Easy," Remnant said softly, steadying me. "You were poisoned by the anthousai thorns, Ri. Xi saved your life."

"Thank you," I muttered, grateful for her support, my eyes never leaving the furious female in front of me. "You're okay..." I breathed a sigh of relief. I had no idea what had happened but the fact that she was here, before me, was enough. I would take her fury any day, for all of my immortal life, to make sure she was always still here.

"Okay?" she hissed. "No Riley Dragoon I am not okay."

Desperately, I reached out, needing to feel her, to reassure myself that she was *alive*, but my hand stilled when she flinched away, disgust written plainly on her face. The sting of it worse than the slap she woke me with.

"Xi—" My gaze trailed over the tear stains on her olive skin, following their path downward, before freezing on the golden collar around her throat. Fear, horror, nausea, loathing, bitterness, guilt...it all hit me like a tidal wave while I stared at the cursed binding. "Fuck," I whispered, licking slowly at my lips, bringing my gaze back to her stormy grey eyes. Both of them. She wasn't even hiding, her furious beauty hitting me and stealing the air from my lungs in a whole new way.

It was a look I had feared seeing every night since The Wailing.

"Please," I said, shifting closer but respecting her need not to be touched by me. Her eyes never left mine, wariness flashing in that grey whirlwind.

Remnant sighed remorsefully, her hands falling away recognizing that the rigidness of my spine and the lack of the putrid poisonous smell meant I was at my full strength once again. "I'm going to scout the area to find our best route from here."

Neither Xi nor I acknowledged her and after a moment's pause she sighed one more time before her footsteps, feather-light, and soon silent, disappeared among the dense foliage.

"You knew." Xi glared at me as soon as Remnant was gone, tears pooling in her eyes, "You knew that I'd rather throw myself on an enemy's sword than to ever feel *owned* again. You know how they treated me. Like an animal to be trained and tethered. You knew!" she screeched.

I flinched, her choice of words that she rather throw herself on *an enemy's sword*, unbeknownst to her, was my undoing. Gruesome memories full of bitterness and rage ripped through me and I spat harshly in her face. "Fuck, Xi. Of course I knew! Except it wasn't you watching *me* bleed out with the goddess's light leaving my eyes was it? No. It was fucking me. I was the one that held your throat together shielding you from The Wailing. I was the one that felt your heart go sluggish, and that beautiful air deplete from your lungs." I shook from my own restrained fury, "I could not do it. I could not let you die, not when I knew I could save you, and I would do it again if that were my only choice."

She lunged for me with a cry, her nails scraping across my skin through the shirt I wore. The sharp pinpricks welcome against the onslaught of emotional turmoil roiling inside us both as she pulled me closer to her, her mouth just inches from mine. "You should have let me die!" she screamed while tears unleashed from her eyes—a fierce storm opening up to drown the world in her despair.

Laughing condescendingly, I snapped, "Just as you let me die moments ago right? You could have been free of me then Xi Lanora Chin. A free fucking pass. With me dead, my possession of you would have ended. So why did you do it?" My chest rose and fell with each passing word, our angry breaths shared, seething through clenched teeth.

"Don't," Xi hissed back, punctuating the words with a push.

I snorted. "Don't what, terrella? Don't tell you that there is never any option in this entire fucking universe where I would sit back and do nothing while you die? Don't tell you that I broke a sacred vow I made to my parents and myself to never use this tainted power? All to save you. Don't tell you that I could not bear the thought of never having you by my side—to never drown in your beauty, crumble to my knees at just your touch, or be awed by your fiery will and insurmountable power? To be honored by your undying, loyal friendship, to lo—"

"Don't," she cut me off, seething just as I was. Her nails leaving thin rivulets of blood trailing down my chest.

I growled inches from her lips, continuing my words even as her eyes begged me not to. "To love till the end of time." Her hands trembled and I reached upwards to slide my own over hers. "I only breathe for you, Xi Lanora Chin. Would you truly deny me the only air I need to live by allowing yourself to die?"

Her anger wavered and understanding flickered within that gorgeous grey, enough that I closed the distance between us, my lips grazing hers. It was her choice, I never wanted it to be otherwise.

Her mouth slammed into mine, and my hands snapped up into her hair, devouring the breath that was rightfully mine, that would always be mine. Possession or not, I loved Xi Chin and it was about goddess damn time she knew exactly where I stood—and it wasn't going to be on the fucking sidelines...not anymore.

CHAPTER 22

H IS LIPS ON MINE felt like bitter salvation. Riley Dragoon was my freedom and my captivity. One was by choice, the other taken. Anger burned through me for seeking out more of his touch, my hands wrapping up into his hair, my body crawling into his lap. Our lips smashed together, both in fury and in need while hot tears still fell traitorously down my face.

Riley said he loved me. But he also *owned* me. I screamed in agony, ripping away and shoving him from me with disgust. At myself, at him. I didn't even care that it sent him sprawling back onto the jungle floor. Furious, I commanded the stone, snapping it around his arms and legs, spreading him like the phoenix wings tattooed across his body. I hated my hesitation as I looked down upon him with mouthwatering need. Waving my hand, I relished the sound of him grunting while I jerked his body into position, bitterly enjoying his look of shock and fury. That beautiful andalusite color of browns speckled with muted greens. The color of enraged earth—my earth.

Well fucking good. He should know how this feels, to still *want* even while betrayed, to still *love* even when deceived.

Both our chests heaved with exertion and pent-up frustration. The weight of the collar around my neck became more obvious with each precious expansion of my lungs—it only served to aggravate me all the goddess damn more. Signaling to the earth beneath Riley, I raised him upright, a sacrifice on an altar and watched as he strained painfully against the restraints.

"I want answers, Dragoon." I forced a step back, keeping myself distant, knowing if I touched him again I would not be able to stop.

His jaw clenched and his eyes glared before a small smile played across his lips, desire mixing with the anger in his eyes. "Then take them from me, Chin."

Narrowing my gaze, I manipulated the stone slab again, stretching his arms higher, smiling back as he winced. "You are clearly not in a position to demand anything, air elemental," I snarled, hooking my fingers under the collar so that his gaze fell on his daming choice—a choice that could very well destroy everything about us.

Riley's nostrils flared and I did not fail to notice that his eyes lingered heatedly on the metal around my neck. "I gave you the one answer that matters the most. I love you."

"Riley this isn't a game! Love does not imprison, it frees!" I shouted.

He shook his head, his smile saddened, not quite reaching his eyes, the sparkle in them gone. "The next move is yours, Xi Lanora Chin."

"How did you hide the collar?" I snapped, denying him the words he wanted to hear. I never even whispered them inside my mind before today, let alone allowed the truth to be spoken out loud. Love was something that could be fractured, abused...*manipulated.* Ever since I escaped my parent's cruel prison, I had decided that I would never allow myself to be so vulnerable again and yet here I was.

Riley sighed, twirling his fingertips in the restraint, and I felt his air brush against the side of my cheek wiping away the trail of tears he saw there before gently swiping back my hair like he always did. "There's blood in your hair," he murmured distractedly, staring at the strands, fear flashing in his eyes before looking up at me. "I can enchant the collar so that no one can see it. You saw the collar my uncle uses because he is a demented soul and relishes the power he has over others."

I licked at my lips, I wasn't sure if knowing the collar could be hidden made me feel any better, ignorance and denial were never a good recipe for a future, if there even was one for us now. "And the leash I saw?"

The darkening of his face told me all I needed, but he answered me anyway, his voice low and dark. "He deserves the darkest pits of Sheol for that. I would never fucking leash you, Xi. I never wanted to possess you in the first place, why in the goddess would I do that to you willingly, and why would you ever believe me capable?"

I pursed my lips, I never truly did, but I needed to hear it out loud, said truthfully in the words of the fae. "What is this power called? How does it work exactly?"

More of his air drew around me and I allowed him to pull me closer before I commanded the earth to anchor me to the ground, stopping just inches from him, close enough to feel his warm breath on my face.

His gaze trailed over it as if to memorize details. "You are the most beautiful creature I have ever seen and I hate the air for keeping the space between us," he whispered as if to himself, words that he never meant to say out loud.

Biting at my lip, I raised my chin, goddess how this fae undid me. But I needed answers.

He sighed again, his familiar breath pleasantly washing over my face, a smell of mint and fresh mountain wind. "My power is called possession. My mother and father had it, as does my uncle. When used correctly it can allow the exchange of energy to amplify one anothers equally." He shook his head, "But the power always designates a possessor and a host and it can be easily tainted. It can be used to force another to do whatever the will of the possessor has. It can be used as an enthrallment."

"Like your uncle," I breathed.

He nodded, watching me carefully. "Like my uncle."

"Why keep me bound, why not release me after I was healed?" I hissed through clenched teeth.

His head bowed and his voice wavered, the truth like a broken prayer escaping his soul. "Fear, shame, guilt, avoidance. Fear because to release you, would also leave you vulnerable not only to our world but also to my uncle. You are a very powerful and cultivated fae, Xi. Leaving you unprotected was something I was not willing to risk ever again." He shook his head. "Shame and guilt because then you would have also known what I had done." His eyes trailed back up to me, studying the kaleidoscope of emotions shimmering across my face. "Avoidance because I never wanted to experience this exact moment, where you look at me like I am a monster—just like my uncle."

Inhaling sharply, I studied the immeasurable agony in his eyes. It was more than just the fucked up situation we were in, the truth of it was deeper than that. "There is something you're still not telling me."

Pain etched into his features as he looked away and swallowed hard, his green hair plastered to his face. "As you know, my uncle was my father's brother," he began slowly, "and he always obsessively coveted my mother. To an extent that was borderline madness. Due to this, he was never welcomed in our home." He paused, swallowing again, "One night, my uncle visited our family unexpectedly while my father was away. You see, my father was a fae that enjoyed helping others. He'd stop anything and everything to lend a hand, and a town nearby had suffered from an abnormal storm. My mother did not wish to go that night so he left me in charge. My uncle saw that as an opportunity—I fully believe that he orchestrated the whole thing, from the storm to knowing my father's weakness to assist others. We should have known he would have stopped at nothing to feed his monstrous desire to possess my mother."

Horror ran through my body like a ghostly chill. "Stop. You do not need to speak of the rest."

Riley's sad hazel gaze snapped back to mine full of resolve. "No, I do. You need to understand that my decision to possess you was never taken lightly. I have not told a single soul this story although I suspect the General knows—but you deserve the whole truth no matter what it may cost me. I owe you that much at least."

My brows pulled together, nodding, my ill-timed humor easing the discomfort we were both in. "We did agree that it was safe to say she knows all."

He snorted half-heartedly before beginning again. "My uncle he...he forced his power on my mother, he was strong and skilled, I was young and untried. He overcame us both and when he possessed her, he was impossible to stop. He used her power to keep me restrained." Riley gritted his teeth, his nostrils flaring with anger. "I have wished so many times that my parents would have used the possession on each other, then he would have never been able to take her and he would have never come. It is mostly the reason why I kept you bound to me—my fear of him taking from me again, something I will not allow. That fucking bastard would have to kill me and extinguish my soul from eternal life before I would ever allow him to take you."

"Ri," I whispered.

His eyes roamed my face and I felt his air smooth out the wrinkles of horror I knew were etched there. It's whispered caress trailed down my face to the tension in my muscles, kneading them until they relaxed. "I'm okay, terrella," he whispered back before his air fell away and he continued the last of his story through graveled words. "My uncle forced me to watch while he controlled her, compelled her to—I could do nothing, not with her power added to his."

My hands reached up to cup Riley's face. "No more, you don't need to say anymore, Ri."

Riley's mouth turned into my hand and kissed it softly. "I need to." His warm breath tickled against my palm. "When my father returned the damage had already been done. After finally getting what he had craved for so long, my uncle cared not to keep my mother. You see you can only possess one fae at a time, and he enjoys the hunt and power of domination, but he is also a fucking coward. He fled before my father could exact retribution and my mother was so broken afterwards, my father didn't dare leave her side." His eyes shuttered closed then, lost in the painful memories.

I pulled his face towards me, kissing his lips softly, giving him the strength he needed to say the rest. "What happened to them Ri? To you?"

His eyes opened and wracked my soul, penetrating it so thoroughly I inhaled sharply. "They made me vow to never use this power on another, and then they fell on each other's swords. Killing one another. The pain and damage my uncle had caused was too much for my mother to bear. They were soulmates, Xi. My father felt *everything* she had gone through, her pain, her shame...he could not live without her and she no longer wanted to live. The fae cannot take their own lives but they sure as fuck can take it from one another and that's exactly what they did."

"Riley—" I stammered brokenly, the choices he made to save me so blindingly clear that my eyes burned and the proverbial weight of the collar lifted. It no longer felt like chains but an adornment of a broken, scarred love.

"Release me, terrella," Ri said, his strong voice fracturing even more, his eyes blazing with torment and devotion. "You are right, this is not a game and I no longer want to play."

CHAPTER 23

T HE EARTH SLID FROM his body, back to where it came from, leaving behind nothing but our still bodies and aching hearts. Unsure, our eyes locked on each other seeing one another in a way we had never done before.

"May I kiss you?" Riley broke the silence, his uncertainty tugging at my weary soul.

I didn't bother answering, instead I closed the distance between us, pressing my body against his, feeling the tension-filled doubt dissolve when I leaned in to kiss his lips.

A soft press, a tentative slow swipe of his tongue, then my mouth parted, an unspoken consent of forgiveness and the telling need for more. But Riley kept his exploration slow, as if I was a new, breakable thing that he needed to savor and cherish, rather than devour and ruin. His hands threaded gently into my hair and my own responded, wrapping up his wide muscular back, moaning softly when his leg pressed into my core, sending a shocking thrill throughout my entire being. There was no stopping my slow grind on his leg. If I had ever desired Riley Dragoon before then this surpassed anything I had ever felt, a fervor instinct that I needed to live.

The soft caress of his hands trailing from my hair down my back made us both groan. Stopping on the soft curves of my ass, he pressed me closer to him. "Xi," he said reverently against my lips, his breath increasing and his hands tightening on my body, trembling from holding back. I gasped when his air suddenly swirled around us in a cyclone of unsuspecting wisps and glittering butterflies, swept up by his violent current. Spiraling in the tornado of air, their colors blurred, cocooning us in a dazzling display that blocked out the rest of the world.

It was beautiful—his power. All violence and enchantment, he wielded it with ease, never wavering even as he slowly licked his way down my body, his breath hovering hotly just above the base of my throat.

Wrapping my hands into his now wind-blown hair, he swallowed hard, kissing the golden ring that was heavy against my panting breaths. "I pray one day, you will see what I have done not as a way to imprison you, but as a symbol of my love, terrella—a covenant of just how far I will go to ensure you survive this forsaken world. To either save or destroy, it does not matter which, but that it is done by *your will* alone."

Planting one last kiss at my throat, his hand curved upwards, trailing over my breasts to hook a single finger through the ring, pulling me even closer, leaving me gasping and reaching for his shoulders. Slowly wetting my lips with my tongue, his andalusite eyes blazed and a low growl rumbled in his chest making my core clench with a thrilling spark of desire.

"I promise you, I will never, ever use this against your own will and should you decide to be free of it, all you need to do is ask. But I won't lie, my terrella, as much as I hate what I have done, this does hold so many interesting possibilities for us." He tugged the collar again. Unable to control my response, I groaned loudly. All I knew now was that suddenly this hard bite of metal on my skin left me feeling more exhilarated than repulsed. He grinned at my reaction, his other hand on my ass forcing me to grind even harder against his body, pressing into his hardness. Long and throbbing, his cock jolted against my touch. "Possibilities that are making me so fucking hard right now," he finished.

My stomach clenched with need and I panted at the image of him moving inside me, holding me in place with both his power and symbol of devotional love. "Show me," I challenged breathlessly. In two words giving him both my consent and my trust.

Raking his eyes upwards, he inhaled, fully expecting me to tell him to remove the possession, something I was not entirely sure I wanted anymore.

I gave him a soft encouraging smile, kissing his swollen lips, whispering upon them a confession I had always been afraid to say out loud, "I love you."

Flashes of color highlighted the sudden bright smile that stretched across Riley's face, while his tousled green hair fell over his eyes. He looked roguish, and savage and wild, and within the safe cocoon of his power I was captivated.

It was breathtaking—he was breathtaking.

Threading more fingers to curl slowly around the collar, he tugged playfully, his mouth brushing across mine, humming. "I know my terrella." Leaning down he gave my lips a whispered kiss, "Now allow me to *show you* just how much I do too."

Nodding, the gold metal around my neck flared, liquid warmth spreading across my sensitive skin, already on fire with desire. "Goddess!" I cried out, collapsing against his hold as the fire inside me turned into a blazing inferno, Riley's shared emotions abruptly colliding with my own.

Unquenchable thirst, insatiable hunger, deep longing ache threaded through my heart followed by exhilarated joy and devotional need that made my body tremble uncontrollably. This was all Riley, this was all of what he held back from me. Tears welled in my eyes and together we crashed to our knees, always in sync, never once out of rhythm, our awed gazes never wavering from each other.

Shaking, my hands reached up to swipe away his windblown hair, falling more into those eyes I loved, and then tracing my fingertips down his face. His eyes fluttered closed at my touch and I panted when my actions created an uncontrollable need that was not my own, provided by the connection the collar gave us.

Riley chuckled at my reaction, taking my hand, he smirked before he started to trail it over his body, watching my eyes widen in awe—overwhelmed by the feel of his pleasure created by my touch. Nothing but ragged breaths escaped me as he drew my hand lower still...over the hard planes of his muscular stomach, sending my own in knots from the dual pleasure and anticipation, right before falling over his hard, throbbing, cock.

Rapture...pure pleasurable rapture unlike anything I had ever experienced before amplified tenfold inside of me, and my head threw back with a scream as my entire body exploded, cumming in such a violent force, that it ripped through my body like a hurricane. It sent me spinning over the edge of bliss and beyond, shattering me with one single touch of my hand over his cock.

Riley roared, drowning out my own screams, and through the haze of uncontrollable pleasure, his body crashed into mine. Our clothes ripped from our bodies in a flurry of imperceptible movement, leaving me sprawled and blinking up at him, his naked body like a sensual god looming over me. A powerful presence that had just given me the most exquisite pleasure I had ever experienced. If this was what it was like to love Riley Dragoon, then he could have me in any way he wanted.

Possession or not.

"Fuck," he breathed, his eyes closing for a brief moment, face contorted with what looked like torturous pain, but there was none in the open bond between us. Licking my lips, my gaze trailed down his toned body that trembled above me and fell on his engorged cock standing high upon his abdomen, cradled on full display by the intricate artistry of his phoenix tattoo. So many times I had been transfixed by the way those wings rippled with each thrust into my body, each drive was a strong downbeat of wings that would send me flying to new heights—and this time I wanted to feel it from him as I watched.

Riley was a metaphor in both power and physicality that left me wanting to be forever wrapped inside his prose. Graceful, powerful, free, and strong. He *was* the phoenix that marked him.

"You didn't cum," I moaned with him at the feel of my hands trailing lightly over his body, my nails tracing the fine work of the feathers over his pelvis, purposefully avoiding his twitching cock that leaked with his desire for me.

Riley released a shuttered breath, the scent of mint and rain washing over me, igniting new sparks of pleasure and drawing a ragged groan from his lips.

"I've had years of practice," he panted, "from holding back from you." Another sharp inhale from both of us when my fingers lightly brushed over the head of his cock, catching some of his pre-cum and smoothing it over my fingertips. "Keeping the distance you needed," his voice was so strained, his chest heaving with gulping breaths, "fucking my hand at night when you took lovers to your bed."

A strong sting of jealousy shot through my heart and I hummed. A small part of me was thrilled that he would be jealous of another except when I did take a lover, I only ever visualized him.

Wrapping my hand around his cock, covering the ringed ink, we both cried out, my core quivering, his dick throbbing, both of us hungry for more. "Well then, let's—" I moaned while stroking him, the amount of pleasure crashing into me from the bond was immense. How the fuck he hadn't cum already when I was on the verge of doing so a second time was goddess damn impressive. "Lets make sure you never have to fuck your hand again Ri," I smirked, bracing myself when my hand reached down to cup his heavy balls, drawing up at my touch, a hissing breath escaping from his gritted teeth. "Unless it's for me to watch, that is."

"Fucking goddess," Riley choked. "Terrella, if you don't use my dick soon, I fear I might die of need, or go wild punishing you." he leaned down to capture my breast in his mouth, biting at it softly before sucking hard. "Mercy or savage, my love. Which will it be?" Rubbing his face against my hardened nipple, I gasped, torturing us both even more when I squeezed his cock—*hard*. Drawing another hiss, and pulling a soft cry from my soul, I guided him to my aching pussy.

"I choose savage, show me your wild punishment."

Rearing, his hand shot to my throat, encasing the collar with it. He thrusted forward, slamming his cock inside me with one thorough stroke, leaving us both moaning and convulsing against each other. My screams of pleasure soon were swallowed by his mouth, muffling his own beastly roar, his body pounding into me with erratic need.

Holding on I met his thrusts with my own, my eyes falling back at the intensity of our combined orgasms. The possession bond revealing just how beautiful and precious such a tie could be when it was one of love.

And his love was a storm unleashed, crashing savagely into me like waves upon a rocky shore. A love only I could bear, meeting his ferocity with my stubborn inability to yield. We were contrary forces, yin and yang, a perfect unison that I could never tire from and never live without.

Hardening again inside of me, feeling the evidence of pleasure between our joined bodies, Riley rolled, positioning me to straddle him, bridging his hips up, planting my bare feet firmly on the ground knowing the way I loved to feel the vibrancy of the earth underneath them. Soft air swept my wind-blown hair back from my face, his eyes gazing up at me with love and wild intensity. Smiling, his large hands reached down to curl around my ankles, holding me in place. "Ride me terrella, let me feel what it means for the earth to take deeper roots through the storm. Like you have rooted so completely inside of me."

I leaned back on his muscular bridged legs, summoning the power of the earth, holding it in my heart for him to feel while I slowly rode his cock, my leverage from the ground making the movement easy to control.

"Fucking goddess above and below," Riley whispered, the winds shielding us speeding with our climbing, fervent release, the colors blurring with each slide of my body against his.

We were one. We always would be. And when we fell, we did it together with cries of love and roars of devoutness that if not shielded by Riley's winds, would have rattled the entire universe.

CHAPTER 24

Remnant

M Y FOOT SLID PRECARIOUSLY onto the swaying curve of the delicate branch as I emerged from the tree canopy out into Faerie's night sky. A soft breeze kissed across my face in welcome and the stars brightened at my upturned gaze. The glow of the three moons joined and I sighed happily, every part of my tired body calming at my return to the dark.

My soul hummed its pleasure while somewhere below, hidden deep in the jungle, behind a cascade of shadow, air and earth, the elementals were also finding what called to their own—the love that beat within their chests for each other.

Extending my hand out to the shadows draping over the trees, I pulled them from their peaceful slumber, their smokey presence flickering and swirling in tribute to the moons. Perhaps it was nostalgia, the memory of my mother and her shadows, that made me impulsively play with the darkness like I had once done with a light heart and no weight on my shoulders.

With ease my hands weaved them up into the stars, honoring the night and its ability to allow reflection until a new day started. And when dawn *finally* dissolved the shadows, a new rebirth would begin. A bright and golden promise that glowed like Faerie's sun, delivering new precious opportunities if only one was brave enough to take it.

Painting them across the sky, the shadows darted, connecting a series of stars that glittered under my concentrated gaze. I smirked when the constellation I had been searching for was finally traced by the darkness, a grouping of stars to the south that hovered above Lacail. Spilling into the night sky, the shadows filled the outline, revealing a great phoenix, spreading its reborn wings over the lands.

I smirked at the irony, fate was such a clever bitch, even while revealing its hand of foreboding guidance, it was still reassuring. For we walked the correct path—daunting as it was. Floating across my admiring gaze, a low smoldering wisp of green and gold pulled my attention back to the canopy and the world below. "Well hello," I whispered, reaching out with an open palm to the curious wisp and smiled when it settled peacefully onto my hand. "Aren't you a unique little thing," I added, pulling it closer to my face to study its coloring. It was rare to find wisps in multi-hues. The green and gold glow of its soft flame was surely a mark of the divine and a sign of renewal. But what it meant for it to choose me tonight and its future purpose were beyond my understanding.

A fluttering of wings and a soft chirp drew my attention to a chickadee hopping along the waving branches and fluttering leaves. A black beady eye turned towards me almost in chastisement, as if being up here put me at great risk. It was worth it, the need to find my heading and a reprieve from the jungle heat trapped below outweighed any fear I had of falling.

Sighing, I gave the nosy bird my own look of admonishment. "And you could not be more obvious," I pointed out, before returning my focus to the slumbering wisp still curled in my hand. Smiling softly, I tickled it gently with my fingertips until the wisp stirred, releasing it back into the star-studded sky.

Green and gold. The thought ruminated inside my mind, as if it were the answer to the riddle that was my life.

Another chirp.

Scowling, my gaze zeroed in on the chickadee once again. "Yes, yes, I know. Time to go." My gaze softened on the tiny creature as I added, "You need not worry so much."

The bird warbled back, and I swore it was the equivalent of a bird snorting, I was sure of it. Tipping its feathered ass in my direction, it launched into the night, disappearing into the stars without so much as a trilling goodbye.

"Is she talking to herself again?" I heard Xi whisper incredulously beneath me.

I grinned, filing away the fact that Xi would never be the greatest choice for a scout. While her earth power gave her the ability to be stealthy, her demeanor rarely was. She faced everything head on—strong and unyielding.

A trait I enjoyed immensely.

"I'm pretty sure she can hear you Xi," Riley muttered.

I snorted quietly. I could hear him too, neither one of them would make good scouts. How they stayed undetected in the City of Light was a goddess damn miracle if this was their way of being inconspicuous. Cool air blew my hair across my face, a nudge to move on. Inhaling deeply, I leaned back with my arms spread wide, gravity taking me head over heels as I flipped silently through the air. The shadows immediately there to cradle me through the zig zag of trees and dense greenery—a free fall of trust, my heart pounding excitedly with the rush of it all.

Landing with not even a whisper of a sound, my eyes opened, glowing in the dark jungle at the unaware backs of the elemental fae still staring up into the canopy. Rising slowly, I held back my laughter when their loud whispers continued.

"I don't care if she can hear us, what is she doing up there anyway? Does she not know where we are? Isn't she supposed to be this all powerful fae? Imagine, the strongest of us not having any sense of direction," Xi drawled.

Riley tilted his head, studying the jungle above. "The general of Faerie must have her reasons for moonlighting above the trees, terrella."

Unable to hold back anymore, I answered sweetly, stifling the laughter aching to be released. "That she does indeed." Jumping with alarm, they turned sheepishly to me. Giving Xi a pointed look, my shadows trailed forward, indicating the path we needed to take. "Lacail is but a few hours walk from here, in case you doubted my navigation skills, earth elemental." Holding out my hand, the shadows returned, dropping a sack into my out-stretched palm. "Yes, you read my mind, my luvs, some food would do us all good, especially the elementals, I do believe they have worked up an appetite now that their other hunger has been sated."

A bright red blush bloomed over Xi's half covered face, but Riley only delivered a dazzling grin. "Food sounds fucking amazing," he cried, surging forward. Quickly, I swiped a piece of dragon fruit from the sack before the air elemental ripped it from my hands without so much as a thank you.

My brows rose high at his desperate rummaging resulting in a low gratuitous moan around a mouthful of food, not even registering what it was he ate.

Glancing at Xi, her nose wrinkled abhorrence. Riley Dragoon currently lacked any manners of a respectable fae, and while she may have found it disgusting, I was highly amused.

Patting his stomach against a clean black leather shirt with matching pants, he spoke through a mouthful of masticated jerky, "Thank you for the set of clothing." His eyes sparkled, "We look like a proper unit now, that is, if you still had your vest, General. Which reminds me," tossing the disregarded leather cord that once bound us in my direction, he smirked when I caught it with dragon fruit still in hand, "I made one for each of us." Waving his free arm, still guarding the sack of food like a dragon, he indicated the black leather bracelet tied around his wrist.

Dropping my head down, I swallowed hard, hiding my emotional gratitude of his extended acceptance and friendship within the dark cloud of my hair. Slipping the bracelet on my wrist and cinching it tight, I cleared my throat, looking back up to see more food shoving grotesquely into his mouth. "Thank you, Ri."

Grunting, he rammed a whole slice of bread into his mouth, answering while chewing. "You're welcome Rem."

Nodding, I cracked open the dragon fruit, careful to avoid staining my new adornment, its sticky juices flowing over my fingers. Biting into the soft flesh of the fruit, the mild sweetness welcoming on my tongue, I glanced up at the elementals, smiling comically at the sight of them. Xi was hovering around Riley, her arms waving around in chastisement as the air elemental danced away from her, sputtering his excuses of relentless hunger for his poor etiquette with wide eyes. I snorted, thoughtfully chewing. Whether my shadows chose black on purpose or not, the color looked good on them—like distinguished soldiers of a legion of darkness.

No, not a legion. Forces. *Shadow Forces.*

Yes, I did like the sound of that. Swallowing, the gnawing of my stomach that I had been ignoring the whole day finally eased as I moved past the ravenous air elemental and his irate partner, hopeful that we would reach Lacail by morning. As much as I preferred the night, I enjoyed facing my enemies in the light so they could see their upcoming demise—a treat I was savoring for three select fae I knew would be waiting for us.

Whirling around me, they sensed my vengeful mood, and draped curling tendrils over my body. Sighing into their cool caress, a hand with the same leather bracelet as mine, suddenly gripped my arm, spinning me back around to meet the solemn expression of Xi. My shock and frustration quickly dissipated into worry as I met her gaze. "What is it? Are you okay?"

Releasing me quickly as if burned, she sighed, "I wanted to say thank you." Chancing a look back at Riley, he glanced up from the bag of food to look at us confusedly. Xi shook her head, growling, "*We* both wanted to say thank you, for saving us. I am unsure what we did to deserve it but we owe you a life debt. Both of us. One we vow to honor."

Recovering quickly, Riley stood straighter. "Yeah," he said through a mouthful of jerky, "fank ye."

I looked between them, a surprising disappointment pooling like a sickness deep in my gut. I never wanted a life debt vow to tie them to me, I wanted a choice, a choice of friendship, as much of a friendship a lonely, abandoned shadow fae could ever wish for.

"Of course, but no need to thank me. I am not that kind of monster, Xi Chin. I don't allow innocent fae to die just because they have personality and passion. Before I was a general, I was just a shadow fae too."

Riley snorted, swallowing his food and finding his proper etiquette once more. "Sorry to break it to you Rem, but you have never been just a shadow fae. We know the stories. Xi has been telling them nightly to anyone who would listen."

I looked between them. Riley's expression full of humor while Xi studied me more closely, a wrinkle forming on the uncovered side of her face.

Giving her my best courtly smile and burying down my irritating sadness, I tossed the unfinished dragon fruit to the shadows.

I was no longer hungry. "Shall we continue? I do believe we have proven to this jungle that they better not fuck with us anymore. The last of our stretch should go smoothly."

I turned my back on them as I walked away, my practiced smile falling with each passing step while my fingers spun the leather around my wrist. It was just a bracelet. I should have known it meant nothing.

"No comment on her tone this time?" Riley asked dryly, obnoxious chewing joining their following footsteps.

I awaited Xi's reply but there was none. Just her assessing gaze boring into my back, only enhancing the terrible pit of heaviness in my stomach.

CHAPTER 25

Lacail. City of Stone—and not just any stone, firestone. The intricately carved gateway sparkled with flecks of yellows and oranges, almost beckoning to be ignited in an explosion of earth and fire. It would have been a welcoming contrast to the silent emptiness that greeted us now.

Something was not quite right.

Worriedly, I passed a look to Xi. It was rare when her eyes did not meet mine, but this time her focus was elsewhere, and I wasn't sure if I should be worried or offended that her attention was stolen from me.

Studying her profile, Xi's brow wrinkled slightly behind the hair that shielded her face, a sign of unease that was directed right at Remnant. The shadow fae's strong stride led us quietly through the still town, her cropped linen shirt billowing in the gentle breeze, her pale skin glittering against the sun beaming down on her more brightly than anything else around us. An honorable spotlight and I half wondered if she was ever aware of Faerie's attention on her or if she had grown so accustomed it was of little consequence.

Turning my gaze away, I frowned at the empty marble-flecked streets that should have been bustling with a new day's morning agenda. Shops were closed with not a single living soul in sight, the air ominously charged as if the entire town held its breath.

"Am I going to be the first one to ask, where in the goddess is everyone?" I said, breaking the tension filled silence and then stilling as shadows slapped coldly across my mouth, cutting off any other comment they thought I would make.

Xi's hair blew out from her face in an aggravated sigh while Remnant spun on her heel, her emerald green eyes shooting through me like a mother scolding a child, a raised finger pressing against her mouth.

Earnestly, I nodded my agreement with more vigor than was perhaps necessary. Anything to get her terrifying shadows off me and a safe distance away, where we could mutually respect one another.

As if noting my wishes, the darkness slid off, pooling at my feet before snaking upwards like smoke from a fire back towards their master. Remnant gave me one last narrowed look but her warning silence was all for naught. I felt the air shift, sharp with something far more treacherous than stinky trolls or anthousai bitches. A long hissing wail soon followed, snaking through the streets, dust billowing upon the marble in its wake, slamming into our still bodies.

Coughing, I slashed the air clean with my power and my stomach churned with unease, unable to register the sound, a sound that did not belong in Faerie, and also regretting the copious amount of food I had just consumed.

Shadows sprung forth, wrapping hurriedly around Xi and I before the entire world blurred. Stumbling they tossed us into a darkened shop, the sun barely providing any light, as Remnant raced through, silently closing the door behind her, eyes still trained on the street.

Reaching outward, I steadied Xi just as the shadows shoved her into me. I could not help but think it was their silent way of telling me to keep her safe. Squeezing her tightly just once, my nose inhaled her fresh scent of river rock and grass before I released her.

Remnant spun towards us, eyes glittering with both worry and adrenaline, speaking low in the darkened shop. "I need you both to listen to me very carefully." Thank the goddess for being an air elemental, shifting blades of grass were louder than her at the moment.

Xi's gaze flickered, meeting mine briefly, before we both hedged closer to the general.

"What is it, Remnant?" Xi's voice a soft flutter of air.

My brows raised, I hadn't realized she was capable. Knowingly, she jabbed her elbow into me, keeping her contemplative gaze on the general.

"The seal to Hell is here and the beasts of origin's prison has officially weakened."

I frowned, glancing out at the empty street. "That sound...it was an original beast?" Quickly, I attempted to recall the stories my mother and father had once told me of the monsters that used to terrorize these lands during the times when the ancient fae were first created.

Remnant nodded.

"What are we talking here?" Xi tugged on her hair. "Slaugh, manticore, cyclops, leviathan—"

I frowned. Outside the air stirred again, this time a crow joining the hiss, and I felt my blood turn cold remembering one very specific story about a half rooster, half snake-like creature..."Basilisk," I breathed.

Remnant's sharp gaze shot through me as she nodded. "Yes, a creature that hunts by sound and scent and is very much *nocturnal*."

I glanced out the window towards the clear cobalt sky, beams of light glittering down on the marbled streets. "It's full daylight outside," I said, pointing out the obvious.

Xi frowned, tilting her head in thought at the general. "You think there is something wrong with it, like the trolls in the cave," she breathed. "And like those trolls, you're going out there to...*help* it."

Wrinkled lines formed between Remnant's dark brows, her pale beauty still prominent even as her lips pressed into a thin line.

A slow breath, like an exasperated sigh I did not know I was holding, escaped me. "Fuck, this isn't exactly troll bowling, Rem. They were not monsters of origin. You know just as much as we do why they are locked away by two goddess damn seals."

Being this close to her, there was no missing the flickering glow of excitement in Remnant Dark's eyes.

"Fuck," Xi reiterated my last words, seeing it just as I had. "This is a bad idea Rem, we don't know how to fight that kind of monster, they are legends only, let alone knowing what its goddess damn problem is."

Her shadows brushed against us and I felt them anchor both our feet to the floor. Looking down at them I growled before narrowing my eyes on my new friend. "This better not mean what I think it does, Remnant Dark."

She gave me a small sad smile and my chest tightened. "There will be no we, just me. You two have a much bigger task, you must find the seal to Hell, it is within this town."

"I'm sorry, what?" Xi gasped.

"I concur, terrella." Narrowing my eyes on the shadow fae, I folded my arms across my chest, "There is no way you think a seal to Hell is more important than you facing down a fucking basilisk, Rem."

Remnant grinned, looking from Xi to me, amusement twinkling in her eyes. It was the same look she held within the Saltu, when the feral gnomes chased us, and when fighting off those psychotic anthousai cunts. Did no peril ever affect her? And how in the Sheol had she survived this long without someone watching her back? She practically searched for danger...a hazard that made it even more miraculous that she was still alive.

"Fine," I murmured slowly to her, "but the moment something goes wrong we are coming out there to help."

Xi's white silky hair swung forward agreeing with me, her hand falling on Remnant's shoulder. "Be careful, Rem," she whispered.

Her brows rose at the worry in Xi's voice and I smiled inwardly—Remnant Dark had won over Xi Lanora Chin. The most stubborn of us all and like the earth that coveted the most precious stone deep in its core, Xi coveted friendships the same way. Fiercely protected for the rarity that we were to her.

A pale hand reached up and covered Xi's, squeezing it gently. "Find the seal," Remnant whispered to us both and then winced when another loud screech mixed with an enormous hiss shook the walls and sent chills of instinctual warning through us all. Swiftly rising away from Xi's affection, the shadow fae made for the door with confident steps, only to turn back with a wink. "Duty calls, oh and by the way," she whispered, "don't look the basilisk in the eyes if it comes for you."

"I don't like that tone," Xi hissed back.

"Shit, please tell me you are not indicating the legends are true?" I whistled quietly.

The glow in her eyes dimmed and she tilted her head behind us. "Unfortunately for this town, the legends are very true, Riley Dragoon." Shadows swarmed around her, releasing their anchors on our person and then she was gone. Only air swirled where she had once stood, just like the first time she left us to fight a battle on her own.

In unison, Xi and I slowly turned towards the direction Remnant had pointed.

"Fuck the goddess to Sheol and back," I swore in sadness and a bit of fear. I was fae enough to admit that at least, since not even a few paces behind us twenty fae stood, petrified in stone with terror etched on every single one of their faces.

"And fuck the death god himself. Sweet goddess Ri, we can't leave her to fight that thing alone," Xi whispered, striding for the door with determination, ignoring the blast of another angry screech that rattled the entombed fae behind us.

I lunged after her. "I agree, terrella, we look for the seal and make sure our General lives to see another day."

Xi nodded, her lips pressing grimly together. "Our General. Yes that sounds about right. She is ours now." A storming, single grey eye shot over her strong shoulder, her tone mimicking the same one Remnant had parted us with. "Time to have some shadow fae version of fun."

Chapter 26

"To your right!" Ri's air whispered along my ear and I ground my teeth to focus on my power and not the hot shiver his breath created.

Slowly controlling the crashing buildings in the distance, I could practically feel Remnant's glaring look of disapproval as the basilisk tore through the city in search of her...or us. That much was still uncertain.

"So any ideas on where this firestone seal is?" Ri breathed again, as we crept quickly along the shadowy alcoves, my power retreating from the landslide of rock deep into the marbled road. It was somewhere below—I could *sense* it. But there was so much of the firestone laid within that I could not pinpoint an exact location.

"Why would they build this goddess damn town from firestone?" I tugged on my hair, stretching my power to feel the ebb and flow of the earth beneath my feet and all around me. "All it takes is one naive wielder to light up this city."

"I find myself suddenly thankful that you are not naive, ter-rella."

I gave him a sharp look and his mouth curved upwards in a half-cocked smile. "You are only thankful *now*, Dragoon?"

Winking, Riley wrapped his air around me, pulling me flush to his body, and I gasped. His heat flooded into my skin, en-veloping me in the safety of his air. "I amend my statement..." he murmured, the mint of his breath a refreshing breeze upon my face. "I am *more* thankful than ever before."

Leaning forward, I closed the distance between us, planting a soft kiss on his smiling mouth, his hand instinctively cupping my exposed face. "So am I, Dragoon..." I whispered, then tilted my head up with a smirk, "For you to raise me up to a better vantage point, that is."

Together we peered up the stone wall of the high tower where a bell hung, hauntingly silent.

He quirked his brow. "An unusual request for you, your feet will no longer be on the ground."

I licked at my lips. "There is too much stone blocking me from finding the artifact. The seal must be pure firestone but I cannot pinpoint it while submerged within the city—"

A finger pressed against my lips and Riley smiled down at me. "The last and only time I've ever seen you this nervous was when we stole the Empedolces staff."

Slapping his finger away, I shot him an annoyed glare. "Ri, she is out there on her own facing a goddess forsaken basilisk, she dragged me out of that Faerie ring alone with her heart bare and untold dark confessions on her lips. All for us." I shook my head, my gaze falling to the ground and I shifted uncomfortably. "It's the least I can do for her," I confessed.

Riley grunted, pulling my chin back up, determination set in his eyes. "It's the least *we* can do terrella. Now hold on tight."

I inhaled at the stirring of his element swirling around us, my hair blowing further across my face before he pressed the full length of my body against his. His chest vibrating with a low groan just moments before he shot us straight up into the air landing whisper light on the tower's ledge.

"Sweet goddess," I gasped, eyes widening at the view of the city and the general just a few streets away. She walked confidently down the smooth marble path, its yellows and oranges glittered like hot sparking embers reflecting in the sun, and not fifty feet in front of her stood the most grotesque and enormous monster I had ever seen. As tall as the building around it, the basilisk's shrill crow shook the city, windows shattering in a spray of glass raining down on its great rooster head. Ending in a hiss, a great forked tongue slithered between a serrated beak full of sharp fangs. Bright red feathers that trailed down its serpentine-like body trembled with its rage, only to be accented by its unfurled leathery wings. Clawing at the street with razor sharp talons, bigger than my forearm, the beast's beak dripped with saliva, burning holes into the stone below. Instinctively, I pulled Ri to me when without warning, it screeched, streams of fire shooting upwards into the air. A warning sign to the shadow fae that faced this creature without fear or hesitation—and without sight!

"The goddess is playing tricks with my eyes," Riley cursed, "please tell me she isn't blindfolded, Xi?"

Unable to lie, I simply stared. Remnant Dark *was* blindfolded and with no weapon in hand. Her only defenses were the shadows licking at her feet like dark flames rising from the depths of Sheol. They set her arms ablaze in shadow, excitedly anticipating their next task.

"We need to get down there—" I hissed right before a streak of violent lightning crossed the cobalt blue sky, drawing our attention outward, beyond the town's borders to the waves of green grasses below. The Goddess plains rippled, and with it, large marshmallow clouds rolled in, thundering upon each other, battling the skies with its great storming wave.

Riley leaned out over the ledge of the bell tower, his gaze fixed past Remnant and the basilisk, his face darkening gravely. "That's no natural storm," he growled.

"Ri!" I hissed, my hand snatching out to grip his thick arm, nails digging into his soft flesh, jerking him back to where the most immediate danger was. That fucking storm could wait—in fact I knew that storm *was* waiting.

"The goddess damn me to Sheol and back," Riley breathed, his gaze turning on what mine could not look away from. Now just feet away from the basilisk, Remnant Dark bowed low, genuflecting to the great beast's monstrous form while the shadows enveloped her body.

Its talons pranced, scraping harshly on the marble under her lowered gaze and a long serpentine tail wound across the street, curling around the bowed shadow fae general who never flinched. Tilting its large beak downward, its tongue slithered out around her head, slathering its acidic saliva upon her, burning holes in her shadow shield—and still she did not stir in fright.

"Is she...?" I brushed my hair back fully, needing both my eyes to comprehend what I was seeing.

"Speaking to it?" Riley finished my sentence, shaking his head. "Yeah, she is, in ancient fae."

I sputtered, my heart racing, when the basilisk beak dipped lower still, its head twitched, cocking sideways to listen. "She is veritably mad. What in the love of the goddess could she possibly have to say to that...that mutilated creature."

Riley snickered, "It's a good thing you're not the one negotiating with a beast of origin."

I licked at my lips, unable to take my eyes away, my breathing short and slightly erratic. "Shut up Ri and tell me what she is saying."

Chuckling still, he bent slightly, his warm breath at the shell of my ear. "She says..." he stalled, inhaling markedly before I felt his lips widen in a smile. I was unable to tear my eyes away from the incredible display of bravery...or was it insanity? With Remnant, I wasn't sure anymore. "She is just...exceptional. The legends don't do her justice Xi."

Grinding my teeth, I dug my nails into his arm harder. "What? What is she saying, Riley Dragoon? Goddess help me, don't make me bury you within this bell tower."

His grin grew wider and for a brief moment I thought I would have to follow through with my threat, but when he spoke it was the words I wanted though not what I fucking expected. "She says, *My great beast brethren, I see your pain and your rage. I know you had no control over the fae you killed here and in the other towns. I have not come to fight you, for you are fierce. No. I have come bowed before you to help you so that I may take your pain away without violence and the cost of more lives.*"

I inhaled sharply, watching transfixed as she rose, her gaze meeting the lowered great eyes of the basilisk. "What? What other towns?"

Riley grunted beside me. "She did say we needed to hurry to get here."

"No. Goddess no." My hand covered my mouth. All those fae...we could have saved them if I hadn't been so foolish. Guilt burned through my veins like the acidic poison dripping from the beast's mouth.

"There was no way we could have known, terrella," Riley said softly, his voice solemn and distant, straying just as mine did with the thoughts of hundreds of fae meeting their end, frozen in stone, because *we* were too late.

Swallowing hard, my breath caught when Remnant's hand stretched blindly outward. Gaze steady, she stroked the fierce beak of the basilisk without hesitation. I did not need Riley's hearing ability to know that she was cooing to an original beast like a babe.

Opening its jaw wide in invitation, her arm disappeared inside the beast's mouth, amongst the serrated fangs. Tail coiling around her defensively, my heart began to pound in my ears right before my hearing was shattered by a blood curdling screech.

I didn't wait. I didn't hesitate. I jumped straight from the bell tower, the air roaring around me while I dropped, the ground rising up, rumbling beneath my feet, propelling me into a forward sprint. "No!" I screamed, watching fire burst around both beast and fae, its brightness blurring my vision. Blindly I continued to run, praying that I was not too late, that there would be something left of the shadow fae that I now had the honor of calling my friend.

When my feet came to a hard stop and my body abruptly pitched forward, I cried out. Reacting on instinct, I softened the earth, weaving it into coarse sand before landing with a muffled grunt, saving my face from being crushed by marbled stone. Sputtering out the gritty earth, I stilled, tasting a unique energy within the ground—a pure, concentrated form of smoldering hot rock.

"You've got to be goddess damn kidding me," I sputtered, thrusting my hand deep into the sand, my pulse thundering in my head. Coaxing the earth to shift beneath, I soon felt a disk-like object, heavy and thick, settling into it. I grinned in the dirt, chuckling madly at my bit of luck—except there was no luck in Faerie.

"Uh Xi," Riley said dryly, "I hardly think this is the best moment for playtime in the sandbox."

Wrenching my hand from the ground, I held out the pure concentrated form of firestone, gold and glittering against the darkened sky where the rolling clouds still waited ominously.

Riley pointed, "Is that—"

"Ah, you have found the seal, well done." Remnant's calm, unfazed voice drew both of our attention forward. A pale arm stretched out to me, blocking my vision. I blinked at the beautiful and precise scrolling tattoos etched along the flawless skin, following it up to Remnant's soft smile.

It was then that I knew I was getting better at reading her—because beneath her bright emerald eyes, I caught a flicker of trepidation before it disappeared into a careful mask.

She wriggled her fingers at me, indicating to take her hand, "I can't help but think you were worried about me, Xi. Apologies for tripping you up. I did not want the basilisk to be frightened by your presence." She tilted her head, "Or were you just looking for an excuse to play in the dirt?"

I snorted and heard Riley's failed attempt to smother his laughter. "I think that is very much an understatement, Rem," I drawled, slapping my hand in her own, the shadows releasing my feet while she hauled me up effortlessly, despite my being almost double her height.

Riley stepped closer to us both, his eyes first scanning her body for injury before turning to the street behind her where one very pissed-off basilisk was now missing. "What in the goddess fuck happened?"

Remnant waved a large fang, forcing us both to rear back from the venom flicking off it. "Rotten tooth. Once I removed it, the basilisk left. I suggested the far southern mountain ranges for its new home. Hopefully the Roc won't mind. They are closely related, you know."

I gaped at her and the tooth she held proudly in her hand, happiness glittering in her emerald green eyes. "Right, they may as well be twins even. I'm sure the eagles would love to know they are comparable to an unsightly half-rooster snake."

Tossing the fang up into the storm ridden air, she chuckled as she watched the shadows hungrily snatch the deadly tooth, pulling it into their dark embrace.

Shifting uncomfortably, my eyes narrowed. "So that's it, then?"

She nodded, biting at her lip before releasing it with a pop. "Yup that's it."

I tugged on my hair, pulling it back across my face. "Goddess help us," I breathed exasperatedly.

"Hate to break up our cute little team bonding moment, but this is certainly not it and there is no goddess who can help us now," Riley said, staring upwards, the rolling thunderclouds we had seen earlier blooming over us. Faerie's cobalt sky faded into shades of deep blue and black, as if the very atmosphere had been brutalized and bruised. Riley had been right before, this storm *was* unnatural but so was the rage spreading across his handsome features. My stomach fell. Our past had caught up with us...in the form of *family* we wished we'd never had.

I narrowed my eyes at the town's gates, sensing her there, waiting. Birth bitch had come to play but this time I would make sure her games ended here.

CHAPTER 27

Remnant

I KNEW XI SAW it, the disquiet in my eyes when she held up the seal of Hell. It wasn't the artifact itself that gave me pause—whatever awaited beyond the gateway of Hell, it hadn't met me yet—no, it was its *unnatural* hiding place.

As if it had been perfectly placed there for the exact moment Xi would fall.

A lucky break, a coincidence—something I sure as goddess never subscribed to. This was fucking Faerie. Coincidences were nothing more than intricate webs of fate, a concept that captured and ensnared those who were not prepared for the cruelty of time to play by a new set of rules.

Rules only its taunting passing knew.

"Well," I said, cracking my neck from side to side, eyeing the growing black sky, the increasing winds swirling my dark hair around my face like my shadows, "I guess it's time for a little reunion for you two, since the whole family decided to stop by."

I shrugged, pulling back my tangled strands and patting my stomach. "Most unfortunate timing. I am starving." On cue, my stomach growled. Goddess, what I wouldn't give for a nice, buttery croissant.

Riley's handsome face twitched, a small smile forming on his lips as he pulled his angry eyes from the sky. "You know Rem," he said, throwing his arm around me, "I just so happen to know a perfect place in the plains where they make the most sinful, hot cuppa tea and scrumptious pudding to go along with it. It's on me, we can share."

Xi walked by, choking with indignation, "Anyone worth calling themselves fae knows that the best thing to order at Pastry Plains is the custard tarts. Don't let him fool you, Rem. He just wants all the tarts to himself. The last time he visited he ordered all of them before anyone else had the chance to eat a single one."

"Not fair," Riley pointed out, "the sticky toffee pudding is delicious." He winked down at me, mischief glittering in his hazel eyes.

My stomach growled again, "I *do* love custard tarts. I am prepared to fight for them if I must, and fair warning, I don't lose. Not when it comes to pastries." I shot a wink up at him.

Riley laughed, squeezing me into his side before heavy winds slammed into our bodies, the storm reaching us as we approached the edges of the town. Its roaring rush muffled Riley's next words. "Don't listen to Xi, there is no need to fight me for them. She's just jealous that I offered to share with you first instead of her," his chuckle carrying on the gusting winds.

I couldn't help but grin back and my heart seized at the image of him—carefree and impish as if the world weren't so dark and heavy, so much like my brother Kade. The sudden and precious memory of my lost sibling was a boon that Riley Dragoon had no idea he had given me. One I would cherish for days to come—the loneliness and emptiness of my life were more obvious than they had ever been before.

"Fair warning general, Riley Dragoon's version of sharing is 90/10. Ninety percent his and ten percent yours, if that."

I grinned at the frown in her tone.

"Lies!" Riley sputtered.

Xi turned around to look at him rolling her eyes. "The fae don't lie, I see through you Riley Dragoon and so does the general." Done with the conversation, her uncovered grey eye targeted the sentient shadows flitting around me. "Hey shadows," she cooed. More than eager, the shadows plunged in her direction like a hungry pet wanting a treat. The delicate sound of unrestrained laughter bubbled from her chest. It was a sound I hadn't heard from her before and it seemed even Riley was caught by the rare moment. "Be dears and hold onto this for me will you?" Without warning, she tossed the seal of Hell into the air. The gold disc glistened against the dark sky before it was swallowed by the thirsty darkness of my shadows.

Satisfied, they curled around Xi's neck, thankful to be of use and basking in her praise, her hand absently stroking their shimmering tendrils.

My heart warmed at the sight, it was the first time Xi had not frozen in terror at the shadows' presence, let alone their touch. By doing so, she had fully accepted me into her life—all that I was and all that I was not.

For I was never going to be a shining beacon of light for Faerie. No. I was always going to be in the shadows, the loner in the darkness, the one that did the things no one else had the heart nor the stomach to do.

But I was also the one that would give the last of my breath fighting for the fae I loved. There was no doubt this friendship was meant to be—how easy it was to laugh and cry in their arms, to rage one second and then be at peace the next, safe within their presence. The fae had a saying for such a friendship.

Amici animae. Friends of the soul.

Something I had never had before and never expected when I set off on this quest. I had asked the goddess what I was missing and she answered in the form of the famous elemental twins of the plains. They were my *amici animae.*

Lightning crackled overhead and if it weren't for the impending battle looming just outside these gates, I would have thought it beautiful against the black and blue skies. Our sure strides slowed against the fierce winds.

"That bastard is really pulling out all the stops," Riley snarled, stepping away from me and slashing his hand downward to create a resistance free path.

Xi's steps came to a stop just past the gates and her lips pressed into a thin line. The wavy grassed plains were now condensed, the winds ripping through and flattening them to the earth. Lightning crackled, striking the ground, setting areas ablaze, the smoke swirling with the relentless storm, joining the large fluffy thunder-head clouds above.

But the violence of the elements destroying the plains wasn't what caused us to pause. Stepping alongside her, I gave the regiment of fae in the distance a lethal look.

"Is it wrong for me to say I am happy it's them?" she whispered over the rush of air and thunder, her hands curling into fists. I could not see Xi's parents from here, but I could feel their slithering evil presence. "I want it over, I want the nightmares to end once and for all."

Placing my hand on her shoulder, I nodded when she peered down at me. Fierce determination etched in the beauty of her face, making her look more like an avenging goddess than a simple earth elemental seeking vengeance. "We will be here with you every step of the way."

Riley growled low on her other side, his gaze narrowing on the one fae that was a blight amongst them all. It was the same figure I was also watching—Rory Dragoon, Commander of the Queen's city forces, was a fae desperate and that made him more dangerous than ever before. "They will attempt to split us apart," he spat.

I nodded, "Yes, with us separate, it will be easier for them." Signaling to the shadows, I sighed, their comforting, dark tendrils curling up along the tattoos of my arms. "But they still will not win, their deaths are marked for this day," I said sweetly.

Xi shivered next to me, "General?"

Pulling my gaze away, I arched a brow at her, "Yeah?"

She grinned madly, shaking her head, white hair catching the wind so I was struck by the full thrall of her beauty. "This time, I fucking love your tone."

CHAPTER 28

XI'S LAUGHTER CUT SHORT, her eyes widening in horror and my heart dropped dead in my chest. Protectively, I lunged for her but it was too late.

"Run!" she screamed, throwing us backwards just moments before the earth fractured. Monstrous cracks and splinters separated the lands, spraying up grass and dirt, and the entire world roared with the force of its great divide.

I rolled upon the trembling earth, Xi's power sending us all sprawling upon the thick grasses battered by both air and the separated earth. "Xi!" I shouted, thrusting out my own power to slow my momentum and grasping for anything that could stop me from tumbling off the edge of the newly formed cliff.

Silver glinted in my periphery, a sword thrown by Remnant's hand, and I honed in on the sinking sound of steel plunging deep into the ground. Contorting my body, I grasped at the hilt of a blade I knew well. Muscles straining to the point of ripping, I roared, falling halfway over the ledge, before momentum ripped me back around.

Inhaling dirt and grass, I moaned, willing my body to stand upright despite every fiber of my being crying out in protest. Hair blowing across my eyes, I swiped it back, peering over the edge into an abyss that could have been my demise.

"Riley!" screamed Remnant, her voice urgent but muffled in the violent winds. My eyes scanned the chaotic destruction. Bolts of lightning and streams of fire poured down from the sky trapping Remnant in a prison upon a small island of earth in the distance. Her shadows whipped around her, shielding her on all sides while engulfing as much of the elemental power as they could, but it was clear she would be overpowered soon. "Not me!" she cried out, already sensing I was attempting to find a way to get to her. "Xi, help Xi!" She waved frantically outward across the great divide where earth still cascaded in crumbling heaps down into a pit of darkness.

Like a polar vortex blistering across the lands, my blood froze when my eyes fell on Xi, leagues away from us, facing two of the most dangerous beings of our world—alone. With her stance firm like the stone she wielded, she missiled rocks towards her parents who stood unperturbed, deflecting each one of her attacks into nothing but dust.

Her parents' assault was pure violence, and within the narrowed space Xi could not avoid their attack, several blows sending her careening backwards. Hair whipping back from her face, her sharp eyes met mine across the great expanse. Grit and anger flared inside of them before they fell on Remnant still holding her own against the multiple assaults.

Separated again. Just like we had predicted but never once had I ever anticipated I'd be forced to choose between my very existence and my pledged honor.

"No," I howled as I slashed my hands downward, the air obeying my command. Rippling from my outstretched hands, it raced towards both Xi and Remnant in a powerful blast that sent Xi's bastard parents flying and snuffed out the flames that kept Remnant imprisoned.

There would be no *choosing*. They were both *mine*. Mine to irrevocably support, mine to cherish with every thundering heartbeat, and mine to make sure that with every breath they took, they soared high above the shambles of this world.

And if I were forced to make the sacrifice, then it would be my own goddess damn self. Never—never would it be one of them, not fucking ever.

Standing here upon the destroyed valley, I made this my silent vow, sending the rest of my power into the fae I loved, seeing her gold collar glow brightly against the dark blue landscape.

"Riley behind you!" Remnant screamed. The opening I had created with my winds now oozed with darkness, and from it another flash of silver shot through the black sky, hurtling towards me with savage, lethal intensity.

A beastly grin spread across my face and I spun, the air following me as I caught one of my scimitar blades as it was launched through the air while unsheathing the other from the ground.

Steel rang, vibrating throughout my arms, meeting my enemy's killing blow. "Hello, uncle." I drawled, taking great satisfaction in the shock rippling across his face. Roaring, I shoved his blade from mine, sending him tripping backwards over the prone, naked form of his captive shifter he had so thoughtfully dragged along with him to these lovely festivities.

A scream of violence ripped from the shadow fae general behind me and my smile grew wider at the thunderous boom that followed shortly after. My uncle's head snapped upward, his normally insipid, pale face growing deathly white...with fear.

Fear that only grew as dark objects fell from the sky—no not objects—fae, dead fae of my uncle's fighting forces. Never expecting him to be this clever of a strategist, I relished the way the general had single-handedly thwarted all his carefully laid out plans. Those fae had been tasked with one purpose only—to kill Remnant Dark. Instead, they were struck down by the lethal explosion of the shadows, an unmerciful deadly blow that demonstrated just how much the commander of the queen's city forces had underestimated her.

The fucking fool.

Blood sprayed and bones were obliterated when one of the bodies hit the ground between us, and I chuckled darkly, the carnage dripping down my face. "You didn't really fucking think you could actually defeat General Remnant Dark, did you uncle?"

Feeling her cool darkness at my back, I poured the rest of my energy into the possession bond with Xi. If I could not be there by her side to fight now, then the least I could do was give her the part of me that could. Blasts of thunderous earth and roaring screams tore across the expanse that separated Xi from us—huge deafening sounds that would have worried me had it not been for the connection I had with her. I could feel her every heartbeat, every breath, every single ounce of her satisfaction, and right now she was smug as fuck with the power I delivered her. This was the beauty of our bond, the reason why I had selfishly kept it, even if giving it did weaken me.

But weak in power did not mean I was frail in strength and right now, I had vermin to exterminate.

Twirling my scimitars, my smile turned feral when Remnant's shadows brushed against my side, their master following shortly after with just a barely imperceptible nod in my direction.

"Commander Rory," Remnant purred, shadows billowing from her body, and swirling across the ground. Their whorling smokey darkness, stretching out to the whimpering shifter who scrambled as far away from them as she could. "I didn't really think it was possible for your tiny brain to piss me off. But consider this," she waved at one of the dead mush of a fae between us, "officially pissed the fuck off."

My uncle snarled, whipping his hair back arrogantly and swiping at the blood staining his face. "Shadow bitch, back off or this cunt dies." His booted foot stepped forcefully onto the retreating shifter's face, pressing her cheek forcibly into the ground.

She cried out in pain, and I instinctively lunged towards him with a snarl, my air slashing outward with the intent to snap his leg in half.

Laughing, he blocked it easily, forcing me to stumble back until Remnant's strong grip stopped me from fully falling on my ass. "Nice try nephew but seeing how you have depleted all your power to your little earth cunt, you are no more a challenge to me than this bitch beneath my foot."

I growled, suddenly caught by the big, light brown eyes of the shifter, greasy strawberry blonde hair falling into their feverish light, her mouth silently begging under the sickening heel of my uncle's boot.

"Please," her breath was nothing but a whisper, but I could hear it, and just like that, the memories I thought I had buried a long time ago came hurtling back.

"Please," my mother whispered to my father, standing in front of him, her eyes void of the light and laughter that used to live free

within them. Her lush strawberry blonde hair fell over her face, brushing against the cold, harsh steel of her scimitar blade.

In front of her, the matching blade to hers squared off, shaking within my father's hold. His long evergreen hair blew in the gentle wind he used to soothe his love, pushing her long tresses back over her shoulder so he could look upon his soulmate's face. His hazel eyes, normally so full of mirth, were wracked with pain, his facial expression that of a broken, fractured male. Grief-stricken, guilt-ridden.

"No!" I screamed, thrashing against the bonds of air they held against me. Tears my mother could no longer form, numb from the days spent spilling them, was not an acute affliction I suffered from, and their hot wetness cascaded freely down my face. My heart beat wildly in my chest, despair and rage filled me. Betrayal became a bitter taste in my mouth from the restraint of air digging into my flesh. The same way they had from my uncle.

My father's sad hazel eyes turned back to me. "I am sorry, my son. I cannot live without her and she cannot go on in this world. She deserves mercy and so do you. This ghost of a life is not what you deserve, Riley."

My chest rose and fell heavily as I stilled my fighting. "What you call mercy I call cowardice. There is still time to heal, there is still time to live!"

"Please, Rilen," my mother begged my soul-crushed father, her gaze ignoring me completely. Turning back towards her, my father's face broke, his own sorrow wetting his cheeks at the way her sword shook violently from being unable to turn it on herself. Something I had seen her attempt many times in the past week. A knife, a fork, the gardening rake, a shard of glass that split her hand wide open. It never worked. A fae could not take their own life and each time she failed, she became more and more of a ghost.

"Vow to me son. Vow aloud that you'll never use this evil power that has cursed our family. Vow you will not use the possession on any other living creature. No matter the circumstances. Vow it, Riley Feng Dragoon. Vow it, on your mother's eternal life."

I sagged in the restraints, now just as broken as the two fae in front of me. There was no swaying them. No stopping this nightmare. "I vow it," I whispered.

"I love you son, your mother loves you too. Now look away, Riley. Look away, my son."

I nodded, swallowing hard, turning my head, and squeezing my eyes shut. My mother's soft whispered, 'please' escaped her lips as *the final sickening thrust of steel penetrated through them both. The air that held me released and I fell. My face buried in the grassy earth as I roared my devastation and anguish out into the universe.*

"Dragoon!" Remnant's warning scream pulled me back from the past and I blinked to refocus, hearing before seeing swords clashing, the glints of silver, the darkness of shadow, and the rush of air whipping around my uncle and my friend, the general.

The shadows billowed out from Rory's violent gusts before they eagerly returned, snapping back into existence to attack him again as he struggled to parry the steadfast blade of Remnant Dark.

She was a dance of darkness. Sliding and twirling along the grasses, flirting with the edge of the canyon's cliff before changing course to begin anew. My uncle grunted with each countered blow, his features straining with both strength and lack of stamina, focusing most of his power on the air he needed to keep her shadows away.

A power he was drawing fully from the shifter female, who lay gasping up at the black sky, tears falling from her eyes, wetting the already greasy strands of her strawberry blonde hair—hair the same color as my mother's.

Feeling my presence above her, I shielded us from the errant winds with the little energy I had left over from Xi's fight.

Light brown eyes beseeched me again. "Please," she said brokenly, "please do it."

My hands gripped the hilts of my dual scimitars. A pair. The right owned by my father, the left by my mother, their essence stained with unseen ghosts upon the shining steel. Raising the right, I brushed her hair back away from her face with my element. A caress of peace and mercy. "To the life given and the life taken too soon, the goddess take you with her golden light to live freely within our hearts where the devoted and young never die."

When I brought my sword down to deliver a quick and pain free death, I did not look away this time. Watching as the golden collar disappeared like the light in her eyes. I had freed her of the torment and torture she had suffered at the hands of my own blood and now I would carry her pain with another mark on my soul.

A slew of curses and damnations descended upon me, my uncle's forceful winds dying and the storm of his clouds began to recede. His voice roared with rage, "Once I am done with this shadow filth nephew, you're next. Now that I don't have that bitch it seems I am free to pick my next prize, and by the goddess that is going to be you Riley Dragoon!"

"I'd pay more attention to keeping your own life, *Commander*," Remnant spat, her emerald gaze burning with the same mixture of fury, remorse, and resolve that was in mine.

Giving me a barely perceptible nod, she attacked Rory at full speed. A rush of steel and darkness blurred together in an array that was pure artistry. She was *fast*—and skilled. Much too skilled for my uncle to have lasted as long as he had. I choked with disbelief, she had been fucking toying with him all along.

Waiting.

Waiting on me to be ready for what must be done. What should have been done a long time ago.

Smiling sinisterly, her sword sliced downward followed quickly by the shadows, powering a blow that ripped a shrill scream from my uncle. His sword fell to the earth with a thud, his arm hanging limp at an unnatural angle, completely fractured. Whimpering and scrambling back, the last of the gusting winds died around us.

His retreat was quickly thwarted by the shadows latching onto him, spinning his body to face me, and when his hazel eyes so much like mine, so much like my father's landed on my face they lit with so much contempt and hatred that it was clear he was just as much of a monster on the outside as he was on the inside.

"Uncle," I drawled, twirling my blades slowly in each hand, approaching him.

"Nephew," he spat, "You don't have it in you, Riley. You couldn't do it in the past when you had the chance and you won't be able to do it now, I am the only family you have left."

I chuckled darkly, stopping the spinning left blade before me. My mother's blade. "I know this confuses you sometimes, uncle," I cooed. Walking steadily up to him, I pointed the tip of the lethally curved blade against his body, watching as his eyes widened and he began to struggle within the shadows' restraints. His air sprung forth, the last feeble effort to defend himself easily thwarted. Sinking my blade slowly inch by inch into his stomach, I chose the most painful way for him to die, relishing in the squelching sound. And when my scimitar finally did puncture through his back, warm blood seeping onto my hand and dripping down to the earth, I leaned in, "But this is the sharp pointed end."

Chapter 29

MY BIRTH BITCH MOTHER laughed coldly, her beauty and finery matching the empty cynical sound. "After all those years you have held us in contempt for *enslaving* you..." she said sardonically, "it seems you could not go without a master after all. Poor child, did I not tell you that your mother knew what was best for you? You could have stayed with us my little earthling, instead of serving under a man that will never understand your element."

My father sneered at her side. "Instead you bind yourself to that...polluted and foul cloud air sniffing *rake*! You are a disgrace to the Chin name, Xi Lanora."

I snorted. I rather liked Riley the Rake, it had a nice ring to it, and my air elemental would enjoy such slander upon his name. Feeling the earth tremble, I began the simple dance I knew was as old as time, weaving fluidly through the whistling stoney arrows sent to impale me from the ground below.

Adding a flourish, a move I had picked up from the shadow fae general, I seized the remaining arrows quivering to finish their task and eased them back into the normal solidity of the earth.

"Happy to see your training at least still holds, daughter," my mother commented dryly, her lip curling slightly with disgust. "Except for that obnoxious display at the end. We may need to double your time on the rack for such lewd behavior."

I inhaled calmly, refusing to rise to her bait. Lowering my hands to ease the continued rumbling storm at my feet and letting the energy of the earth guide me, I drew upon more of Riley's power, a euphoric burst of vitality that sharpened my senses. I could feel everything—everything that graced this world's surface, from the gentle touch of the sky kissing the ground, to the depths below, where firestone gathered under my parents' feet. The fragments wouldn't have been of any consequence before, barely enough for me to induce any particular damage, but with Riley's connection, it would be my parents' undoing.

My eyes snapped open, the sun splitting through the retreating storm clouds, bathing me with its warmth and encouragement. I grinned, knowing Riley and Remnant had been successful and now—now it was my turn for vengeance.

"My dear, I do believe our poor daughter is deranged," my mother said, watching me with disgust. Her brown eyes, so unlike mine, rolled while she plucked at her long, billowing silk sleeves, her features pulled taught by her frown and the severe bun perched atop her white head. It was her signature look because it revealed her elegant bone structure, or so she always told me while she implored that I do the same. At least then, she stated, I might be half as beautiful as her.

Unlike my composed mother, Fuchai, my dickface of a father, spat disdainfully, his dark brown eyes flashing villainously. "A damned waste of all those years we spent training her, Xizi." Pointing a long, tapered finger threateningly at me, he sneered, "The moment we break your little ties to the air sniffer, you will regret the day you were born child! You have brought great shame upon your mother and me."

"Indeed, this foolishness will end today." Xizi raised her arms as discs of stone rose from the deep earth to hover, spinning in her hand. Discs I knew she loved to carve with serrated edges just for her sick enjoyment. As if being severed by a stone disc wasn't already bad enough.

I rolled my eyes. "Please Mother, you could at least come up with something new. Something a bit more creative."

The cunt grinned before snapping her fingers, and the discs burst into flame.

Firestone. She was wielding firestone.

"Ah Xizi you really are a fool," I laughed, feeling the softest caress of Riley's air, and the cool brush of Remnant's shadows as both of them swiftly flanked me, a sentinel on each side. But the shadows were not so rigid, breaking formation in greeting, licking up my legs, shimmering with happiness to see me. Laughing softly, I cradled them up into my arms like a sweet little kitten.

Perhaps having a cat one day would be nice.

My father's face contorted with uncontrollable abhorrence. "You are a disgrace, nothing but a blight on the Chin name!" he raged.

And I laughed, nuzzling the shadows just to see if it were possible for him to choke on his own revulsion. The thought had merit.

"Terrella," Riley's air caressed my cheek, brushing playfully over the strands of my hair, "You are playing with them. Light them up, earth baby. I'm *hungry*."

"I can't say that I am *that* kind of hungry for you Xi," Remnant added dryly, "but if my stomach growls any louder I might be mistaken for a shifter." Remnant patted her stomach before she tilted her head at my mother, fake concern drawing her brows together. "You don't look so good Xizi. Are you ill?"

Screaming, the discs flew from my mother's hands, stepping forward with each one, she hurled them not only towards me but also at my friends. I knew her games and I had played by her rules long enough. If Remnant Dark had taught me anything, it was that games were won by stepping off the chess board and making your own goddess damn playbook.

Summoning the energy of the firestone discs, I burned their energy brighter, exploding the stone into nothing but clouds of dust that rained down on us like fiery ash.

Riley snickered, "Well done, terrella," and with a flick of his hand, the dust concentrated around Xizi Chin, covering her finery from head to toe in nothing but thick, smoking sand.

"How dare you, you ungrateful brat!" sputtered my unfortunate sperm donor who created me. "You shall rue this day. You think your life was insufferable before, I will make it so—"

The sound of my mother screaming frantically cut him off when I re-solidified the firestone around her, encasing her in the very earth she sought to destroy me with. Fuchai roared, always daft without my mother to guide him, he dashed towards her.

"No get back you fool—" she screamed at him, her eyes wide with alarm likely more for her own self-preservation and not his life, either way, it did not matter.

I raised up my fingers. "You should have been more wary of the unsuspecting, of the fragmented, of the impure. For when they join together...they are an unstoppable force, like the rarest of stones, stones that burn." Taking one last look at my mother's frantic brown eyes, I snapped my fingers, "Goodbye birth bitch."

A sudden rush of air encircled us just moments before the firestone lit up in a massive fiery blaze, the bright flash forcing us all to shield our eyes, and the shadows to curl deeper into my arms. My mother screamed but the sound was quickly engulfed by massive explosions that rattled my bones. Looking back, I watched as the earth sprayed upwards from the deep, the firestone below igniting into a mushroom cloud of flames and stone, incinerating my parents into nothing but floating embers.

I should have felt sad, disheartened, maybe even remorseful knowing that they were gone, killed by my own hand, but all I felt was relief and safety. The feelings spread warmly throughout my body and I sighed at the exquisite feel of it—-not sure if I had ever felt such peace in my entire existence.

When fingertips grazed against mine timidly, I looked down to see the tattooed arm of the shadow fae general reaching out, her leather bracelet brushing my own. Without hesitancy, I threaded my fingers through hers, squeezing gently with gratitude for the powerful bond growing between us. We had been alone, but now we all had each other—three of us lonely together.

Sensing our moment and never one to be left out, Riley slung his heavy arm over my shoulder, dragging both Remnant and me inward to watch the continued destruction inside our shelter. The fiery ash cascading over our bubble of air, sizzling out before it even met the mangled earth.

After a moment of silence, Riley snickered. "Hey Rem, what do you call earth elementals exploding?"

I groaned under Riley's arm, tugging my hair back across my face. He always did this, when the emotional discomfort got too great. "Don't do it, Rem. Just don't."

Remnant chuckled, "I don't know Ri? What do you call exploding earth elementals?"

"A Faerie large earthquake."

Remnant giggled and then hummed, nodding with mock solemnity, "A Faerie misfortune indeed."

I blew out a long sigh. My hair fluttered outwards from my face as I dipped away from their warm embrace, and horrendous humor.

"Oh yes, one might even say they were Faerie functional dynamite." Riley burst out laughing and Remnant joined him, her laughter echoing across the canyon both beautiful and haunting.

Turning I regarded them both, clutching their sides, snorting and howling way too hard for such terrible jokes before wiping tears from their own eyes and then starting anew the moment they caught each other's gazes.

My lips pulled into a small smile, seeing the love and loyalty of true friendship between them. After all, Ri did see in her early on what I could not, refused to see—she was one of us.

"Ri, I got it, I got it!" the general gasped between laughs, elbowing him in her excitement. "It was a fae-eruption of epic proportions!"

My brows rose in disbelief, their roaring amusement almost as loud as the explosion only moments ago. High fiving each other multiple times and stomping their feet in fits of hilarity, their snorts and giggles continued.

I crossed my arms with mock sternness while my lips trembled, attempting to hold back my own chortling, they were ridiculous, "You two jesters just about done? I thought you all were on the brink of starvation?"

Their laughter cut short.

"Food yes, we need food," Riley whined, dramatically, clutching his stomach, his eyes wide as if he were suffering a great pain.

Remnant's stomach growled loudly on cue, adding to Riley's hungered agony—a fierce, low growling sound...just like a shifter.

This time, it was my turn to laugh.

CHAPTER 30

Remnant

OUR LAUGHTER DIED WITH the winds. Solemn and quiet, we hiked back through the treacherous grounds of the canyon, coming to a halt at its edge to peer out across the wide abyss where the city of Lacail still stood. Perched perfectly on an island of stone it would be inaccessible for any fae unless they could fly and even then, they would be entering a tomb.

Another permanent mark upon my soul carved next to so many others. Each one representing my failures and the bitter guilt superseding them. I yearned to return Faerie to her former glory—a time that was not scarred by death and war. A time when we lived as one with the lands, the beasts, the skies, and occasionally played when boredom took us to the human world.

But that dream was slipping away like the dust still falling from the sky, and yet each morning, when my eyes greeted a new day, I locked away my fear of failure to start my task again.

The coming of daylight forever mocking—never bringing me the warmth and peace I so desperately ached for.

My eyes narrowed at the lone chickadee, flapping furiously away from the eerie city, the soft ring of the bell tower resonating its haunting summons across the great expanse.

Sadly, there was no saving the fae there. Although we had found triumph, innocent lives still paid the price.

"Xi?" My voice was strong...steady. My sadness and self-sabotaging thoughts forcibly locked away now, enclosed in a vault, deep within my heart, where no fae could ever find it.

"Yes, General?" Xi replied, her tone solemn while her eyes traced the profile of my face. I dared not look at her, for if I did, she would see within the monster that was needed to make hard decisions—and my monster was not for the world to see. For once unleashed...it would surely be the end of all fae.

"Bury it." Emotionless, this was the price of playing in the shadows—of being born to darkness where death always resided.

The collar around Xi's neck glowed brightly in my periphery, Riley's voice breaking as he fed her the power she needed to eliminate this town forever from the plains. "Take what you need, my terrella," he encouraged Xi, who sighed heavily.

Not tearing my eyes away, even while the earth shook and great sheets of stone crumbled from the cliff's edge, I watched as Lacail split from its great pillared island. Gently, Xi commanded the entirety of the city to float within the cobalt sky of Faerie. The sun now setting low, the daylight moved onward to coalesce with the night as it always did—unfailingly so—except this time it seemed to slow, mourning for the fae that died here. Together both sun and Lacail submitted to the darkness, though one would rise again, and the other would stay—respectfully buried deep within the grave of the canyon's abyss.

Above me, the soft sound of a downward stroke from a snowy owl, swooped up into the moonlight, as if it were tasked to carry the souls lost here to the promised gates of Sheol.

***

Full. We were full.

Having traveled through the night, bedraggled and tortured by Xi's tales of the epic sweets that awaited us at the Pastry Plains, the three of us stumbled into the quaint bakery. Half starved for pastries, still covered in carnage and grime, we gave one Sheol of a shock to the poor fae behind the counter and scared half the customers away.

When the owner, Bess, recovered, we were met with the ire of a mother hen. Pecking and shooing us off, she demanded we clean up before we even thought about tarnishing her good name, and her food with such utter disrespect ever again.

Driven by the mouthwatering smell of her baking and borderline fear of the baker herself, we sat refreshed and clean with three cups of steaming hot tea in front of us. A tray, where two dozen custard tarts once sat, was now shoved to the side, not even a crumb to be found on its reflective silver platter. Xi had been right, they were the best tarts I had ever tasted, and even full to the brim, I still craved more.

But my hunger receded when I nodded subtly to the shadows. It was time. "You have fulfilled your end of our bargain," I began, the shadows oozing across the table between us, "and now it is time to fulfill mine."

Xi and Riley glanced at one another warily before peering back down at the shadows dissipating from the worn, rough table, leaving behind the *real* Empedolces staff. Gleaming in the sunlight pouring from the window, its sacred polished wood was like a sparkling jewel lying in the dirt. Reverent and alluring, its power invoked full command of the room—and of the elementals within it.

Barely breathing, Riley and Xi leaned in towards one another, never taking their eyes off the staff.

"I'm going to need the one you stole back," I said slowly.

A pair of hazel eyes and one grey snapped up to me. "Do you hear it too?" they both said in unison before turning to one another wide-eyed.

A small smile danced across my lips, still amused by how perfectly harmonious they always were with one another. I shook my head. "I hear nothing, but then again, I'm not meant to." But I knew *who* was. Controlling the accelerated beating of my heart, I tucked my wavy, black hair away from my face, before leaning forward with commanding eyes, "Touch it."

Xi's hand shook, the first to respond, and then she paused to look towards Riley. Smiling, he placed his hand on top of hers, his eyes glittered with love and devotion as he whispered encouragingly, "We are one, terrella, we always will be." Guiding each other's hands down to the artifact they held their breaths.

The root flared to life the moment they touched it, colors of blue, grey, orange, and gold rippled across their bodies, glowing brighter and brighter until it consumed the room—fully immersed in the stunning color, vibrant with life and energy.

This...this was what it was like to behold the power of Faerie, but just as we began to bow in deference to its greatness, the power disappeared, snuffed from the room like a burning flame.

Gasping, Riley and Xi snapped their hands away from the staff, staring at one another with wonder and fear. Their chests heaved, both unable to speak.

Standing, my chair scraped softly against the wooden floor, I bowed my head low to the newly crowned Lady and Lord of the elemental fae. The true leaders of their people and now...a target for the wrath of the Queen of Faerie. "Well met, Lady and Lord of the Elemental Court."

Xi licked at her exposed lips, her eye flickering up at me, then snapping back down to the staff, "I—no this has to be..."

"A mistake," Riley choked, finishing her statement, nodding furiously.

"Yes, a mistake, there is no way we could be—" Xi's voice broke off into a small cry.

Riley's air wrapped around her, tucking her hair back from her face, and soothing the sudden trembling of her body. The sharp bite of panic and doubt could practically be tasted and I wished I could say it was unwarranted. That there was no chance in this goddess damn universe where I would ever let harm befall them, but fae could not lie.

"It is no mistake," I said softly. "You asked me once how I knew it was you in the City of Light," I gave her a sad encouraging smile, "I see aura's Xi and both of yours flare like stars in the sky, a quality I have not seen from any other fae before. I did not know what it meant then, but I do now. It is the mark of the goddess, the mark of the true leader of the elemental court. She has chosen you both. You sought the Empedolces for it to crown your next ruler. To find the leader that would free your people from the harsh reality of the queen's rule but *you* had it within yourselves all along. It called to you, not the other way around." I sighed and shook my head at how fucking cruel fate could be. "The way I see it, you now have two choices." I held up my finger, "One, you announce your claim of the elemental court without the full power of your people behind you and likely fail. Or two, you wait, you gather your resources, you find your allies, you learn your enemies, and you infiltrate the system from the *inside*. You play a different game."

Xi licked her lips and I could see the burning question in her eyes, one I had asked my own self many times over.

"Ask," I said, my stomach twisting in knots.

Looking between us, Riley frowned but remained silent and Xi fidgeted in her seat, quietness holding the room before she summoned the courage to speak.

"What about Deirdre? You are the General to the Faerie Throne. Your vow is to her and yet you will help us? What about your...*relationship*?"

I could not blame her for asking the same questions I have wondered myself, and as such she deserved an answer. *A real one.* Spreading the shadows around the room, I caged us in our own cocoon of darkness to speak freely, for the first time in two hundred years. "Be at ease, the shadows are to prevent anyone from overhearing the truth I am about to tell you." I gave them both a small encouraging smile. "When I joined the crown, it was because my mother and court had been ripped apart by bloodshed and loss. Something she had sheltered me from and as such, I was uninhibited by the ghosts of the past and was a dreamer of a new future. Deirdre was dangerous and her enormous power called mine, power that made us both outcasts of our own courts and we found solace in each other as a result. I did not anticipate falling in love with her, and if you asked me even now if I still love her, my answer would be yes."

The shadows shimmered around the room, attempting to comfort the bitter regret and sadness I felt at admitting that truth out loud and at the way Xi and Ri stiffened at my confession.

Taking a deep breath, I pulled a shadow from the floor up into my hand, cradling it like a dark wisp sent to comfort me on the twisted path I chose. "But that love between us, it is a dying flame, one that dims with each passing day and each time another fae hangs on the walls of the city." Closing my fist, I met their attentive stares, concern for themselves or for me I was unable to distinguish. Tilting my chin high, my voice was firm and true. "Know this. When I made my vows, my oaths to the crown, it was to the Faerie throne and her lands—not to a *queen*. I have done this *alone* within the presence of enemies and foes, playing the games of heathens and monsters, masked behind beauty and splendor, and I have done it all for these lands—the fae within them."

The shadows snapped promptly back from the walls at my beckoning and licked up my brands to deliver what I requested of them. Curling my hand around the items, I leaned upon the table, the roughened, worn surface abrasive upon my skin. Hair falling around me in a dark curtain, I slid my hand across the surface, the sound of soft tinkling and scraping echoed in the tension-filled room—then silence.

Exhaling softly, I uncurled my fingers and lifted my hand, watching as they both bowed in unison to look upon what I had revealed.

Glittering in the soft morning sun alongside the staff, two delicate silver pins lay. Manipulated and strenuously molded from silver of the Argentine caves, they resembled the smokey tendrils of the shadows that were always a part of me. Made from a dream, they were a symbol of trust and friendship, of loyalty and un-breakable bonds, of the vengeful beast and the resilient beauty that lived in the shadows.

"The choice is yours," I said softly before turning away, swallowing hard. The acidic burn of the unknown rising in my throat while I took the last few steps to the door.

They would need time—time to weigh the consequences of a decision that would alter the course of their very future, likely putting their lives at even more risk. It was for the best that I walked away now.

Grasping the knob of the door, my eyes falling on the leather cord tied on my wrist, I swallowed hard again. I could fucking do this. I could walk away. I was used to being alone and I could still find another way to restore Faerie without them. I just needed to—

The door ripped from my grasp with a forceful wind and my booted feet spun back around, to the inner sanctum of the room. Blinking, I found Xi and Riley standing before me, and I stilled when my gaze fell upon the silver shadow pins anchored on their shirts, flickering in the sun-filled room. The Empedolces staff was left discarded and forgotten on the table behind them.

In unison, they knelt on one knee, bowing their heads, speaking as one. "We pledge ourselves to you, Remnant Dark, in both this life and the next, as our general, our leader, and our friend. We vow to always remain by your side, together, in whatever way the universe will have us."

Riley's hazel eyes peered up at my shocked expression, his wavy green hair flopping over his brow, and he smiled. "You need not be alone anymore Rem."

Xi's uncovered face, also looked up, her eyes bright and focused. "We are *amici animae*. Friends of the soul and we are better for it."

A wide foolish smile spread across my face and I fell to my knees, leaning into them, our foreheads touching as we laughed nervously. "I accept your vow but you need not kneel to me. We are equals," I choked out, "and I also vow to always uphold the trust you have given me as both your leader *and* your friend."

"We accept," Riley grinned, pulling away to ruffle my hair playfully. "So what's next oh great war general of Faerie?"

Xi groaned, shaking her head, leaning back on her heels. "What's next is another hot bath and a week's worth of sleep at the very least."

I snickered, "You might need to hold that wonderful plan for another day." Eyes sparkling, I held up the note that had been burning a hole in the shadows ever since they returned from the City of Night. "This is what's next."

Tugging her hair across her face, Xi cursed. "Goddess help us. There's that tone again. You heard it, right Ri?"

He nodded, rubbing his hands together, the air swirling around them eagerly and his eyes gleamed. "Oh, you bet I did. It means another round of troll bowl, here we come!"

Laughing freely, I felt the strands of fate begin to unravel but this time I would not face it alone, and for that—I would be patient.

EPILOGUE

Morta

I KNELT ON THE destroyed remains of the City of Light, staring numbly down at the mountainous rubble and the frayed leather bracelet in my hand. The sharp, jagged marble cut deep into my knees the same way loss sliced open my heart, and I clenched my fist around the broken leather. I was fucking bleeding out, but on the inside, the loss of Remnant Dark drowned me in an abyss of grief.

I barely heard the sharp commands and barking orders of the shifter fae around us. The only thing I was aware of outside of this pain was that Xi was with me. Fucking goddess to Sheol and back, I swallowed hard. She could have been here, buried beneath the destruction where our beloved general likely lie.

Days. We had spent days digging through it all, with both power and our own hands that broke open and bled and then healed again on repeat. Desperate to find one fae beneath. One living soul. But there were none.

There was only *her* leather bracelet, shredded and scorched, a testament of what had happened here, and I clutched onto it with wretched desperation as if it would bring our general back to us.

Xi's exposed grey eye caught my own, a flicker of hope burning within them and I looked away, narrowing my gaze at the massive shifter looming over us. His body looked just as broken as we all felt. Deep blue bruises and half healed wounds that still bled littered the once smooth bronze muscle, dark circles of fatigue strained around his fierce and bright golden eyes. Seemingly, too exhausted to brush back, his hair fell across his face as he wavered. Quickly supported by the fae who had captured us at his side, the healer accompanying him scanned his body—healing what he could. But from what I could see, hidden deep within the golden one's eyes, there was nothing that would heal those scars even if the wounds did close.

Nothing here that is.

But this *golden one* did say he believed she was alive before he stared off into the distance with both longing and pain, need and desperation, like a lost lover, vowing to find her. To bring Remnant Dark back home.

Home.

We had no home now. Everything we had worked for, the sacrifices we made, the times we held our tongue watching our beloved friend be abused and subjugated by the queen all for the goal to free Faerie from her rule, was gone. And so was our sole purpose. There would be no fae left to even be free, no elemental court to lead, not after today.

We had lost. We had lost everything. *She* was our everything.

The crunching of heavy leather boots in front of me drew my attention back to the present and discreetly I tucked Remnant's leather bracelet away. Gaze traveling up massive muscular thighs encased in tanned leathers to a bared torso covered in tattooed ink, I swallowed. Trailing that ink, I followed the exquisite detail all the way up to the top of his head. A tapestry of art permanently etched into every defined groove of his savage body. Muscle rippled when he crouched his heavy form in front of me, meeting my studious gaze with violent purple eyes that gripped my soul.

A brow pierced with a heavy barbell arched amusedly at my deepening scowl. "So you're shadow forces huh?" His voice was low and gravelly, dark and beastly. A dangerous tone that had me shivering despite myself.

The petite one who found and *captured* us snickered. Her deep brown eyes flashed brightly with knowing and despite her stature, it was clear that she was not to be mistaken for anything but powerful. "Stop playing with your food, Tyr."

Penina. The *golden one* had called her Penina.

Snarling, I broke the corded bonds around Xi and I's wrists with a slice of air, and lunged, barreling into the grinning, unsuspecting shifter.

Fuck him.

Pinning him to the ground with air, a knee on his throat, and a dagger in hand, Xi guarded my back. Her earth trembled beneath us all and I smiled darkly. "Yes. We are *the* shadow forces, shifter. You got a problem with that?"

His returning growl cut short, his eyes widening, and nostrils flaring, I stilled at the sudden delicious scent enveloping me. A deep warmth, something clicking into place inside my chest. An intense need, a *desire*.

Violet eyes began to dissolve into dark heady hunger and I knew then that the great shifter's reaction was similar to mine. His deep resonating purr sent a hot spike of exotic thrill into my bloodstream and my breathing increased.

Our eyes locked again...a reaction like this could only mean one thing.

Soulmates.

Stunned, I followed the way his tongue licked slowly and sensually across his lips, the glint of another silver piercing flashing in the sunlight before he growled darkly. "Riley."

Gritting my teeth, I braced against the hot possessive tone of my name on his lips, ripping myself away before it could fully take me.

"Fuck!" I snarled, whirling from him and turning instantly to Xi. Her own eyes were wide with shock, having felt everything through our own bond, a connection we never closed from each other, not since Lacail but still we kept it hidden. She looked away, new agony joining her raw grief, cutting through me just as quickly as a newly sharpened blade.

No. No way in Faerie was I allowing that to happen.

Walking away from the shifter who was slowly rising from the ground and ignoring his shocked friends around us, I reached for Xi and pulled her into me, slamming my mouth down on hers. Devouring her lips with what I knew would never, ever change, making sure she felt it in every aspect of my being through the bond.

I loved Xi Lanora Chin and no soulmate bond was going to tell me otherwise.

"You're mine terrella," I whispered across her now swollen lips, a sight that made me preen with pride.

"But Riley..." she began.

"No," I hissed. "I am not about to lose you too—not you too. We already lost her. I can't—fuck Xi, I won't survive it." My body shook holding her and the soulmate connection I had felt for the giant, tattooed shifter was gone, bringing back our combined overwhelming grief. Slipping my hand into hers, I brought it to my lips, kissing it softly. Directing my air, I watched her eyes fill with tears as our general's bracelet rose between us and I tied its frayed fragments around her wrist, next to its twin. "Remember. We are one."

Her pooled tears fell from her uncovered eye, staining the olive skin of her gorgeous face, uncertainty flashing within even as she whispered, "And we always will be."

AFTERWORD

I sincerely pray to the goddess that you enjoyed this journey into the past of our beloved shadow fae, Remnant Dark, and the story behind her steadfastly true friends, Riley & Xi.

Hopefully, I will meet you all again in the shadows for the final installment of the Remnant Archives, book 3, Shadows Eternal. Until then may the shadows keep you safe and the gnomes forever piss on your flowers.

xoxo
B.K. Cavaleri

ACKNOWLEDGEMENTS

There are some very special, beautiful humans I would love to extend my heartfelt gratitude and thanks for the completion of this novella.

First Ali, thank you for sticking with me through my chaos and for being willing to take on the role as my author PA. I would have surely drowned in this project if it were not for your steady hands and words of encouragement to guide me through. Everything about us has been kismet since the beginning when we shared our dreams out loud to one another and its mind boggling to see how much we have both grown.

Second, Megan. My little slasher gnome. The goddess blessed me with your passion for an amazing story and fervent need for a solid plot. Your beta reading and proofing took me by storm and I am better for it. I can't wait to see where your new editing business takes you and hope that you will drag me along with you.

Third. To my ultimate hype girl Nat. The first reader I ever had that picked up my book, Shadows Lost, and hasn't stopped screaming it to the world since. It has been my utmost pleasure to have you as a beta and alpha reader on this project. Your feral screams are bar none and I am so thankful to have you in my life. We are in this together my friend.

Fourth, to my feral gnome army, my archiver street team. This book was the first one that you have been with me on from start to finish. Your guidance and encouragement got me through the bad days of uncertainty and I am grateful for your commitment to my dreams.

Lastly, but never last in my heart. Sarah. Your unwavering support, love, encouragement, and drive to make sure I keep pushing my limits is immeasurable. You bring life to these stories with your keen editing skillset and simple but effective "rewrite" statements. I will never be able to express just how much it means to me to have your continued support. I would surely be lost without you.

I lied, that was not the last. I cannot end this book without saying thank you and I love you to my husband. Nicholas, without you in my life this dream would have never even been a spark in my mind. From your gentle whispered words of encouragement and the nights you took on single parenting, to the sweat you poured into making sure I have my first author office to write in, you have been the fuel that has kept this dream alive, you are my Emon, my soulmate, my eternal. Thank you for protecting my heart and my dreams, and making sure that if the world burns around me, I will still have a laptop to write in it.

ABOUT THE AUTHOR

B. K. Cavaleri is a dreamer and storyteller living in Michigan with her husband and two rainbow baby boys. She works as a doctor of physical therapy by day and a writer by night...that's her moonlit vibe when the babies are sound asleep in their beds and hubby is entranced by The Office reruns. It's during that time she gets to dream amongst the stars and make it come to life on paper. It seemed a shame to keep it all to herself, and her characters are much too loud, so she has decided to step out of the shadows and release her stories to the world. Thank you for joining her on this journey.

Want more?
You can visit here and subscribe to be an ARCHIVER for monthly newsletters or to find social!
https://www.bkcavaleri.com/
signed copies available at
www.bkcavaleriarchives.bigcartel.com

ARCHIVER UNIVERSE

Remnant Archives

<u>Shadows Lost</u>
<u>Shadows Ascend</u>
<u>Shadows of Air and Earth</u>
<u>Shadows Eternal</u> (coming soon)

Avalon Archives

Not ready to leave this world? Neither am I. Stay tuned for the return of some of your favorite characters with the introduction of Avalon's story.